SHORES OF WONDER

BUBBA'S SEAFARING SECRETS - WHERE EVERY WAVE BRINGS DREAMS TO LIFE

MAHESHWARA SHASTRI

Made with ♥ on the Notion Press Platform
www.notionpress.com

To My Loving Family

Without your support, encouragement and belief in me, this book would not have been possible. You have been my inspiration and my motivation throughout this journey and I am forever grateful for your unwavering love and faith in me.

To my parents, thank you for instilling in me the value of hard work, perseverance, and dedication. Your guidance and wisdom have shaped me into the person I am today.

To my siblings and their spouse, niece and nephew, thank you for being my biggest fans and for always cheering me on. Your enthusiasm and excitement for my work have kept me motivated and driven.

To my spouse, thank you for your patience, understanding, and unconditional love. Your support and encouragement have given me the strength to pursue my dreams and achieve my goals. This book is dedicated to all of you, with all my heart and gratitude. I hope it brings you joy, inspiration, and a sense of pride in what we have accomplished together.

With love and appreciation,

Maheshwara Shastri

Contents

Foreword

In the divine radiance of Lord Krishna's blessings, this book unfolds. May his wisdom and grace guide your journey through these pages, illuminating your path and filling your heart with eternal light. Embrace the teachings within and allow them to transform your life.

Preface

In a strange but not surprising way, I would like to inform the one who hold this book in their hand, must be alive at this exact moment, taking breath, sensing the touch, feeling something in their minds and by this time, your heart had pumped few millilitres of blood all over the nerve system.

You know all these things, but you didn't know any of them. You didn't make the decision to be you, neither did your parents. You didn't know where you came from and you don't know where you will end up. Your first breath was unknown to you, just as your last breath won't be known either. You think that you are aware of everything, but believe me, you don't. You think you can make decisions about anything in life, but you never know that your life is already predetermined. The reason you are here isn't just by accident, instead it is because you are supposed to be here. You are here as planned, the plan with no error, the plan with the highest precision.

Have you ever wondered who set your life in PRECISE?

What if you could explore the predetermined precision over the course of your life?

Close your eyes and imagine you are ZERO; your size is a trillion times smaller than the smallest species on this planet. Take a moment to imagine, and then begin reading.

We hope you enjoy the journey of Shores of Wonder.

The act of travelling involves being directed to a destination at a specific time and with a predetermined schedule. Almost everyone enjoys travelling, even the youngest of them, who wants to travel with others. Similarly, everyone looks forward to visit their favourite places. Some may say they are not able to travel; they may feel exhausted and stressed if they travel too much.

It is a fact that every human being has to travel at least once in his or her lifetime. Every living being must go on journey. What if journey has no end, no specific place, or no time? Yes, I am not telling you about a trip to a wedding or vacation. I am telling you about the journey of life which begins nine months in advance, with waiting lists of hundreds of thousands, as a toddler crying, looking at the first love of our mother, and it's called the journey of life.

We are on a journey, our home is a vehicle, our father is the driver and manager, and my mother sits in the corner of the car, telling me stories until my station arrives, enjoying every aspect of that ride and serving as a good guide along the way. A mother's love and affection will never be forgotten and their debt will never be repaid.

It is said that as soon as our own stations arrive, we must descend. After we get off, the vehicle will continue on to drop off others, A human being is always in a vehicle of life, the story is about how he landed at his station while no one could see him and what he was battling for next.

Maheshwara Shastri
Author

Acknowledgements

Writing a book is a solitary endeavour, but its creation is a collaborative effort. I am deeply grateful to all those who have supported and inspired me on this incredible journey.

First and foremost, I want to express my heartfelt appreciation to my family, whose unwavering encouragement and understanding sustained me through the long hours and creative challenges. Your love has been my anchor. I extend my gratitude to my friends and colleagues who provided valuable insights, feedback, and motivation. Your contributions have been instrumental in shaping this work. I am indebted to the dedicated professionals who assisted in the production of this book, from editors to designers, whose expertise elevated the final product.

***Cover Page Image credit goes to Lothar Dieterich Germering/ Deutschland,* Thanks a lot Dear Lothar Dieterich** Finally, I want to thank my readers, for it is your interest and engagement that give purpose to these words.

Thank you all for being part of this adventure.

Maheshwara Shastri

Gratitude

Dear Notion Press Team,

I am writing to express my heartfelt gratitude for the incredible journey we've embarked on together. Working with Notion Press has been a profound and rewarding experience, and I am immensely grateful for your unwavering support and dedication.

From the moment we embarked on this literary adventure, your team has consistently demonstrated a passion for publishing, a commitment to quality, and a relentless pursuit of excellence. Your expertise, guidance, and attention to detail have been instrumental in bringing my vision to life.

I appreciate the collaborative spirit that you've brought to every aspect of this publishing process. Your responsiveness to my questions, your willingness to accommodate my ideas, and your timely communication have made this journey not just productive but enjoyable.

It's a rare privilege to work with a publisher who understands and respects an author's voice, and I have found that partnership in Notion Press. Your support has allowed my words to reach a wider audience, and for that, I am truly grateful.

I look forward to many more successful collaborations in the future. Thank you for your professionalism, your dedication to the art of publishing, and for being the conduit that has allowed my words to reach the world.

With warmest regards,
Maheshwara Shastri

Prologue

Amidst the endless expanse of the ocean, where every wave carries whispers of dreams and secrets of the deep, we return to the world of "Black Dots." In our first journey, we explored the enigmatic tales of lives connected by destiny's invisible threads. Now, in "Shores of Wonder," we find ourselves standing at the brink of a new adventure.

This book, "Bubba's Seafaring Secrets," serves as a bridge between those black dots, connecting the fragments of lives we encountered before. Here, in the salty embrace of the sea, we continue to unravel the stories, mysteries, and legacies that began in our first voyage.

As we set sail on this new chapter, let the waves remind us that dreams are never truly lost at sea. They wash ashore on these shores of wonder, taking form and guiding us toward the conclusions, resolutions, and revelations we seek.

So, my dear readers, prepare to embark on this voyage once more, for the secrets of the deep and the echoes of the past are intertwined with the future. Let the sea breeze carry us forward, as every wave brings dreams to life.

Welcome back to the world of "Black Dots," where the journey continues, and where, amidst the shimmering sands of time, we find our way home.

CHAPTER ONE

UNCHARTED WATERS

Long ago, the days were incredibly realistic, and imagination was shockingly vivid; reality concealed itself, and fascination adorned every face. In a world thirsting for knowledge and brimming with kind-hearted souls, a unique bloom was emerging.

Bubba was born to Nerissa and Morvane, a couple who had made their home on the coast of Karnataka's Tulunadu region.

Nerissa considered herself blessed as the wife of a fisherman, dedicating her life entirely to Morvane, her husband, and their beloved son, Bubba.

For the brave fisherman, Morvane, who spent most of his days navigating the coldest waves of the Arabian Sea beneath a scorching sky, the entire ocean was his universe. Morvane worked daily on a Persian fishing boat off the coast of Karnataka.

His career endowed his life with greater meaning. Even as an ordinary boat worker, he was the ships unofficial captain, a technical expert in boat-related matters and fishing techniques. The owner of the boat witnessed a double-digit increase in production and revenue due to Morvane's ideas and suggestions during fishing.

When Bubba turned seven, it was a joyful day for him. He eagerly awaited his father's return, knowing what to expect: gifts, cake, and chocolate, as is customary for children.

On that special day, Bubba's excitement was palpable. The young boy inherited his father's fascination with the ocean and its mysteries. He often joined his mother, Nerissa, as she patiently mended fishing nets, anticipating her husband's return.

The sun began its descent, casting a warm, golden glow over the coastal village. Laughter of children echoed through the narrow streets as they played games, their bare feet dancing on the soft, sandy shore. It was a simple life, but one filled with love and shared dreams.

As evening approached, the villagers gathered near the shore, awaiting the return of the fishing boats. Bubba stood at the water's edge, straining his eyes to catch the first glimpse of his father's boat. Today, his father had promised to share an extraordinary story from the sea, a promise that had fueled Bubba's excitement throughout the day.

Finally, in the distance, the lights of the fishing boats began to twinkle like distant stars on the horizon. Bubba's heart raced as he watched the boats draw closer, one of them being his father's. Morvane's boat was adorned with bright, colorful flags, a sign that they had enjoyed a successful catch.

As the boat reached the shore, the villagers rushed to help unload the nets. Bubba, however, could hardly contain his excitement and darted towards his father. He was enveloped in a warm, salty embrace as Morvane lifted him high into the air.

"Did you catch the biggest fish in the sea, Father?" Bubba asked with wide, eager eyes.

Morvane laughed heartily, ruffling his son's hair. "We might not have caught the biggest fish, my boy, but we have a story that will make your heart race."

With the villagers gathered around, Morvane began his tale. He described a day filled with relentless waves and treacherous winds, a day when their nets had ensnared a remarkable discovery. Instead of fish, they had hauled aboard a crate, sealed with markings they couldn't decipher.

Curiosity piqued, Bubba listened intently as his father continued. Inside the crate, they found ancient scrolls, intricate maps, and a mysterious, ornate key. The discovery had ignited the crew's imaginations, and they now held in their hands the potential to unravel a hidden treasure's location.

The villagers marvelled at the story, their faces reflecting a mixture of excitement and curiosity. The potential of discovering a long-lost treasure filled the air with an infectious energy. Morvane's boat was quickly transformed into the heart of a new adventure.

Bubba couldn't believe his luck. The prospect of accompanying his father on this thrilling quest sent his heart soaring. His dreams of exploration and wonder were about to become a reality as he and his father prepared for an adventure that would take them far beyond the familiar shores of Tulunadu.

Little did they know that this was just the beginning of a journey that would uncover not only the secrets of the past but also the hidden potential within themselves, The real treasures lay in the bonds they would forge, the lessons they would learn, and the legacy they would leave behind on this extraordinary voyage.

Their adventure was about to unveil the hidden face of the world, where dreams and reality intertwined, and where every discovery revealed not just the wonders of the world but also the mysteries within their own hearts. Nerissa gently shook Bubba, her fingers brushing his tousled hair.

"Bubba, it's time to wake up," she whispered, her voice a soft, soothing melody.

Bubba stirred in his sleep, his dreams slowly fading like mist in the morning sun. He mumbled, still half lost in his imaginary world, "Just a few more moments, Mother."

But Nerissa persisted, knowing that the day ahead held real adventures of its own. She leaned closer and spoke with a touch of warmth and urgency, "Bubba, the sun is rising, and the village waits. It's time to greet the day."

Slowly, Bubba opened his eyes, the vivid dreamscape of hidden treasures and sea-bound quests giving way to the cozy reality of his room. He blinked, adjusting to the morning light filtering through the window.

Nerissa smiled, her love for her son radiating from her eyes. "Good morning, my dear." Bubba returned the smile, still caught between the worlds of dreams and wakefulness. "Good morning,

Mother." With a gentle push, Nerissa encouraged Bubba to get up and begin the day. Though the dreams of grand adventures may have slipped away with the morning, the promise of new, everyday wonders awaited outside their home, in the heart of their coastal village.

As Bubba rose to meet the day, he couldn't help but carry a piece of his dream world with him. The hidden face of the world still beckoned, filled with the mysteries of the ocean and the magic of imagination. And who knew what real-life adventures lay just around the corner, waiting to be discovered in the embrace of the waking world?

Bubba's eyes sparkled with hope as he looked at his mother, his heart filled with the anticipation of finally celebrating his birthday. "Mother, will Father bring a cake this time, like he promised last year?" he asked, his voice tinged with excitement.

Nerissa gazed at her son with a mixture of love and sadness. She knew that the promise from the previous year had been made in a moment of optimism, but their financial situation hadn't improved. In a tender, hushed tone, she began to explain, "Bubba, you know your father works tirelessly on the fishing boat, but the sea can be unpredictable. Sometimes, we don't catch as many fish as we hope for, and it's difficult to save money for things like cakes."

Bubba's hopeful expression began to waver, and he furrowed his brow. "But the other children have cakes on their birthdays, Mother. I've seen them."

Nerissa held her son's hand, her heart heavy with the weight of his expectations. "I understand, my dear, and I wish we could have a cake just like them. But remember, we have something more precious than any cake — we have each other, and the love of our family. Your father may not be able to bring a cake this year, but he brings something far more valuable every day – his hard work, his dedication, and his love for us."

Bubba's disappointment lingered, but he nodded slowly, understanding the sacrifices his father made for their family. "I know, Mother. I just thought this year might be different."

Nerissa hugged her son tightly, reassuring him, "Every year is special in its own way, Bubba. Today, we'll find a way to celebrate your birthday with the love and warmth that we have. Let's make this day memorable in our own unique style."

With those words, mother and son shared a moment of connection, reaffirming the strength of their family bonds. Though the cake remained out of reach, their love and resilience would be the sweetest ingredients for Bubba's birthday celebration.

The sun dipped lower in the sky, casting a warm, golden hue over the coastal village. Children's laughter and excited chatter filled the air as they played games on the soft, sandy shore, their eyes frequently scanning the horizon. It was the time of day when the villagers gathered near the water's edge, eagerly waiting for the fishing boats to return.

Nerissa stood among the group, her eyes shifting nervously from the sea to her son, Bubba, who stood apart from the other children, gazing intently at the approaching boats. Her heart ached with worry, knowing that Bubba was eagerly awaiting his father, Morvane, and wondering if he would bring a gift this year.

Morvane was an incredibly hardworking fisherman, and he never failed to provide for their family, but the uncertainty of the sea sometimes meant empty-handed returns. Nerissa had seen this situation before, and she knew that her husband would be met with disappointment in his son's eyes if he returned with nothing to offer.

As the boats drew nearer, their colorful flags fluttering in the salty breeze, Nerissa's heart raced with anticipation and trepidation. She knew that Morvane was a man of his word, and he had promised Bubba a special surprise for his birthday. But the sea was unpredictable, and the catch was never guaranteed.

With a deep breath, Nerissa clutched her son's hand and whispered, "Bubba, no matter what your father brings back, remember that he loves you more than the treasures of the ocean."

Bubba nodded, his eyes never leaving the boats, a mixture of excitement and worry in his gaze. Nerissa hoped that Morvane's return would bring not just fish but also the joy and love that would make Bubba's birthday truly special.

As the boats finally reached the shore and the villagers rushed to help with the catch, Nerissa and Bubba held their breath, waiting for the familiar sight of Morvane. The moments that followed would reveal not only the day's catch but also the depth of love and understanding within their family.

Morvane's heart was light as he stepped onto the shore, carrying a large basket filled with gleaming fish, his face adorned with a wide, jubilant smile. The day had been bountiful, and he couldn't wait to share his joy with his family.

With the boat's ropes secured and the fish safely stored, Morvane didn't waste a moment. He ran towards Nerissa and Bubba, who were waiting with bated breath. The villagers noticed his hurry and watched with curiosity as Morvane approached his family.

Nerissa's eyes met her husband's, and she saw the exhilaration in his gaze. Bubba's face lit up with anticipation as he saw his father rushing towards them, carrying the promise of a special surprise for his birthday.

Morvane knelt before his son, the basket of fish beside him, and whispered, "Bubba, you've waited long enough for this day. I may not have a cake, but I have something even better."

With that, he reached into the basket and pulled out a beautifully crafted, wooden fishing lure, glistening in the sunlight. It was carved to resemble a fish, intricately detailed and painted with vibrant colours.

Bubba's eyes widened with amazement as he took the gift into his hands, a sense of wonder washing over him. "It's perfect, Father! Thank you!"

Nerissa watched her husband and son, her heart warmed not only by the thoughtful gift but also by the love and pride she saw in Morvane's eyes. It was a day of celebration, not just for Bubba's birthday but for the tight-knit bonds that held their family together. The villagers, witnessing this touching moment, couldn't help but smile. They understood that while Morvane may have brought fish from the sea, the real treasures were the love and unity that surrounded Bubba and his family on this lovely day by the shore.

As the night descended upon their humble home, Nerissa and Morvane sat together, their voices hushed in the dim candlelight. Bubba, curious yet unobtrusive, lay in his bed, unable to resist eavesdropping on his parents' conversation.

Morvane's face bore a shadow of sadness as he spoke, "Nerissa, today's catch was better than most, but it was barely enough to pay the rent for this place. The sea provides, but it also demands."

Nerissa's eyes glistened with understanding and concern. "We've always managed, my love. We have each other, and that's what matters most. But I can't help but worry about our Bubba's expectations. He's growing, and he sees what other children have."

Morvane sighed, a heavy burden weighing on his shoulders. "I wanted to make his birthday special, to give him something more than we usually can. That gift I presented today... I didn't really have enough money for it. I had to make it seem like I earned more."

Bubba, hearing his father's confession, felt a mixture of emotions. He appreciated the beautiful fishing lure, but he also understood the sacrifices his parents made to make his day special. He silently vowed to appreciate their love even more.

Nerissa reached out and held Morvane's hand, a tender smile on her face. "It's not the value of the gift that matters, my dear. What counts is the love behind it. Bubba knows that you love him, and that's the greatest gift of all."

In his bed, Bubba closed his eyes, grateful for the family he had and the love that bound them together. That night, he drifted off to sleep with a heart full of understanding and a profound appreciation for the sacrifices his parents made for him.

CHAPTER TWO

A SON'S PROMISE

The sun had barely begun its ascent when Bubba awoke the next morning. He quietly slipped out of his bed, determined to make a difference. He didn't want his father to bear the weight of their family's hopes and dreams alone.

He tiptoed into the kitchen, where Nerissa was already preparing breakfast. Bubba approached his mother and whispered, "I want to help Father, Mother. I want to be a part of his struggle."

Nerissa smiled, touched by her son's earnestness. "You are already a great source of joy, Bubba. But how would you like to help?"

Bubba's eyes shone with determination. "I can mend the nets and help with other chores. I want to ease Father's burden, so he doesn't have to pretend we have more than we do."

Nerissa hugged her son, her heart filled with pride. "Your father will appreciate your help, my dear. We'll work together as a family, and together we'll face whatever challenges come our way."

The stage was set for Bubba's commitment to his family's well-being. With the dawn of a new day, he embarked on a journey of shared struggles and triumphs, ready to stand beside his father in their life on the coast, where every sunrise brought new hope and new possibilities.

Morvane, aware of the financial strains his family faced, decided to make the most of the two days when he wasn't out at sea. He walked down to the nearest boat garage, a place he was familiar with, and offered his services as a mechanic. The garage owner welcomed his help, knowing Morvane's skills were invaluable.

As Morvane worked diligently on a boat's engine, a man of considerable wealth and influence entered the garage. He was impeccably dressed, and his demeanour exuded authority. The garage owner, who was always cautious about his reputation, greeted the wealthy man with respect.

The rich man, however, had a reputation of his own – as someone who wielded power ruthlessly. He pointed at a boat that had recently been serviced, claiming that the repair hadn't met his high standards. He demanded a full refund, threatening to use his influence to harm the garage owner's business.

The garage owner, torn between upholding his reputation and avoiding the wrath of the wealthy man, hesitated. Morvane, who had overheard the heated exchange, felt a sense of injustice. He knew that the garage owner had provided excellent service, and it wasn't fair for him to be coerced into giving a refund.

With determination, Morvane approached the garage owner and said, "I stand by the work we've done here. It's of the highest quality, and this man's demands are unjust. Let me speak on your behalf."

The garage owner, grateful for Morvane's support, nodded in agreement, Morvane then turned to the wealthy man and calmly but firmly explained that the work on the boat was indeed top-notch. He pointed out that the issues the man was raising were minor and unrelated to the garage's service.

The wealthy man, unaccustomed to being challenged, was taken aback by Morvane's unwavering stance. After a tense moment, he reluctantly agreed to pay for the service, realizing that his attempts to manipulate the situation had failed.

As the wealthy man left the garage, Morvane's actions garnered the admiration and respect of the garage owner, his fellow workers, and the customers who had witnessed the confrontation. They saw in Morvane a man of integrity and courage, someone who stood up for what was right even in the face of adversity.

For Morvane, it was a moment of reaffirmation. His actions that day were not only a testament to his character but also a promise to himself that he would do whatever it took to provide for his family honestly and with dignity.

After Morvane's stand against the wealthy man, Bubba couldn't help but feel inspired by his father's unwavering principles and his willingness to take action. As Bubba watched his father work as a mechanic in the boat garage, he began to understand the true meaning of integrity and the importance of doing what was right.

With his father's lessons in mind, Bubba decided that he wanted to contribute to the family's well-being as well. He saw an opportunity when he noticed a rich man's boat docked at the harbour. Without hesitation, he approached the boat owner and inquired about the possibility of working as part of the crew.

The rich man, impressed by Bubba's determination and sincere attitude, offered him a chance. Bubba was thrilled to have secured a job, and he promised himself that he would work diligently, just like his father, to make the most of this opportunity.

Bubba had learned an important lesson that day – the disparity between "want to do" and "I did" often boils down to a single action taken without delay or procrastination. With this new understanding and his father's values as his guiding light, he was ready to embrace the challenges and rewards of his own journey on the coast, where each moment brought the promise of growth and the chance to make a difference.

Bubba's determination to contribute to his family's well-being had led him to seize the opportunity to work on the rich man's boat. However, he was still young and inexperienced, and he had much to learn about the life of a fisherman.

On the day he was to start, Bubba arrived at the harbour before dawn, eager to prove his worth. The boat was larger and more imposing than he had anticipated, its wooden structure towering above him. As he stepped onto the deck, the reality of the open sea loomed vast and daunting.

Unbeknownst to Bubba, the boat he had boarded was destined for an extended fishing expedition, venturing far beyond the familiar shores of his village. The rich man's vessel was known for its ambitious voyages, seeking greater catches in uncharted waters. The crew, mostly seasoned fishermen, gave Bubba curious glances. They could see the determination in his eyes, but they also recognized that he was inexperienced and unaware of the challenges that lay ahead. Bubba's innocence and enthusiasm touched their hearts, and they decided to take him under their wing.

As the boat sailed further from the coast, the sea became rougher, and the vastness of the ocean stretched out in all directions. Bubba, initially exhilarated by the adventure, soon realized the magnitude of the journey. He watched as the seasoned fishermen cast their nets, working tirelessly under the unforgiving sun.

Days turned into weeks, and Bubba's determination was put to the test. The physical demands of the job, the relentless sun, and the ever-changing moods of the sea took their toll. He missed his family and the safety of the familiar village he had grown up in.

But as the journey continued, Bubba's respect for the sea and the fishermen deepened. He learned the importance of teamwork, the art of casting and hauling in nets, and the rhythms of the ocean. He also realized the invaluable lessons his father had taught him about integrity.

Bubba's adventure had taken him far from the village, but it had also brought him closer to understanding his father's struggles and the significance of the family's unity. With each day at sea, he grew stronger and wiser, and he silently vowed to return to his family with a newfound appreciation for the life they led and the sacrifices his father made.

Little did Bubba realize that this unforeseen voyage would not only unveil the treasures of the sea but also uncover a deeper comprehension of Bubba and the enduring bonds that connected him to his family.

Bubba's initial belief that the boat would soon return to his village had allowed him to embrace the new experiences on board with enthusiasm. He had worked alongside the seasoned fishermen, eager to prove his worth, and had formed deep friendships with the crew. The sea had become his school of learning, and the boat his second home.

However, as days turned into weeks and the shoreline remained nothing more than a distant memory, the unsettling reality began to dawn on Bubba. This was not a short adventure; it was an extended voyage that would keep him far from his family and his beloved village.

One evening, as the sun dipped below the horizon, Bubba found himself standing alone on the deck. He gazed out at the boundless ocean, its depths shrouded in the fading twilight. The comforting routine of his previous life had been replaced by an overwhelming sense of isolation.

Shock and anxiety coursed through him as he realized the full extent of his predicament. He was adrift in a vast expanse of sea, far from the familiar sights and sounds of home. He missed his family terribly and yearned for the safety of the village he had grown up in.

His newfound friends among the crew noticed his withdrawal and concern. They approached him, their faces reflecting empathy and understanding. They explained that the voyage was indeed long and challenging, a pursuit of greater catches in uncharted waters. While they sympathized with his desire to return home, they encouraged him to embrace the journey and its valuable experiences.

Torn between his loyalty to his family and his commitment to his role on the boat, Bubba grappled with the complexity of his situation. The wisdom of his father's lessons echoed in his mind, guiding him to face challenges with courage and integrity.

As the boat continued its voyage into unknown territory, Bubba's journey of self-discovery had just begun. The boy who had once been content by the village shore was now navigating the uncharted waters of the sea, an unexpected odyssey that would transform him and deepen his appreciation for the enduring bonds that connected him to his family.

Every night, as Bubba settled into his makeshift bunk on the fishing boat, his thoughts and dreams would carry him far beyond the creaking wooden deck and the rhythmic ebb and flow of the ocean waves. While the boat rocked gently, his imagination embarked on its own adventures. In the realm of dreams, Bubba became an intrepid explorer, his mind unfettered by the confines of the boat. He would venture deep into the heart of the ocean, discovering hidden treasures, long-lost shipwrecks, and enchanting undersea worlds. The treasures that glistened in the depths were not just precious gems and golden artefacts but also the stories and secrets of the sea.

One night, he dreamt of a mystical underwater cavern adorned with radiant corals, its walls adorned with tales of ancient voyages. The vibrant marine life would dance around him, revealing the secrets of the deep, whispering tales of mermaids and legendary sea monsters.

In another dream, Bubba found himself on a tropical island, the soft sand beneath his feet, and the scent of exotic fruits in the air. He explored lush jungles, discovering hidden chests of treasure that held maps leading to even more distant horizons.

With each dream, Bubba's heart swelled with the thrill of adventure. He would wake each morning, briefly disoriented by the reality of the boat's cramped quarters, and then remember the wonders of the night before.

His fellow crew members, observing his nightly escapades, saw in Bubba's dreams the same spark that had inspired them when he first boarded the boat. They recognized that he carried a unique gift—an unbridled imagination that could turn the monotony of the sea into a world of endless wonders.

As the days turned into weeks and the boat journeyed further into uncharted waters, Bubba's dreams served as a source of inspiration and solace. They reminded him that adventure could be found not only in distant horizons but also within the limitless bounds of his own mind. His dreams were his escape, his refuge, and his promise that, no matter how far he roamed, his imagination would always be the compass guiding him back to the treasures of the heart.

The night was dark, and the storm had swept over the sea with an unexpected ferocity. The fishing boat, once a sturdy vessel cutting through the waves, had become a fragile plaything of the tempest. The wind howled, the rain lashed like whips, and the sea raged with an uncontrollable fury.

Amidst the chaos, the fishing boat was tossed about like a leaf on the water. Bubba, still dreaming in his bunk of underwater adventures and treasures, was jolted awake by the calamity. Panic gripped his heart as he realized the dire circumstances.

In the dim light of the storm, he could see the terror on the faces of the crew members as they fought desperately to regain control of the boat. But it was a battle they couldn't win against the wrath of the elements.

With a deafening crash, the boat struck a hidden reef surrounding one of the small islands. The impact was devastating, tearing the vessel apart. Within moments, it was swallowed by the churning sea, along with its crew. The storm was merciless, and the sea offered no evidence of their existence, save for the roiling waves.

In the chaos and darkness, Bubba clung to a piece of debris, a small wooden boat that had broken free from the wreckage. Unconscious and battered, he drifted on the turbulent sea, a lone survivor in the aftermath of nature's fury.

Hours passed before Bubba finally regained consciousness, his body bruised and battered, his mind disoriented. As he awoke to the eerie calm after the storm, he realized that he was adrift in an unknown expanse of sea, surrounded by nothing but the vastness of the water.

His heart heavy with grief for the crew who had become his friends, he clung to the remnants of the boat, wondering how he had become the sole survivor of this maritime tragedy. He felt the weight of solitude, a solitary speck in a boundless sea.

With his village far from his reach, Bubba's journey had taken a devastating turn, thrusting him into a new chapter of his life filled with uncertainty and an uncharted path. As the first light of dawn broke over the horizon, he knew that the days ahead would be a test of his resilience and a testament to the enduring bonds that connected him to his family, even in the face of unimaginable challenges.

Bubba, now known as Hubris, stood at the crossroads of a pivotal decision. He had learned about the greater mission of Black Dots, a mission that went beyond the confines of his previous world. The realization that the fate of humanity hung in the balance weighed heavily on his shoulders.

As Hubris looked at his former co-workers who had come to entice him back to the ship, he understood the gravity of his choice. He knew that returning to the ship would mean living under the oppressive rule of Scorch, a life with no real freedom and the continuous manipulation of their thoughts and actions.

In contrast, the path offered by Eoan, Ken, and Broad represented a glimmer of hope. It was a chance to regain their independence and take back their lives from the clutches of tyranny. Hubris believed in their cause, and he knew that supporting Eoan's mission was the only way to break free from the chains that bound them all.

With determination burning in his eyes, Hubris firmly declined his co-workers' offer. He could see through the illusion of false promises and the facade of safety they presented. Instead, he chose the path of truth, resilience, and the pursuit of a better world.

As Hubris took the first step on this new journey, he also understood that he was not alone. His choice to stand with Eoan and the Black Dots would connect him with a group of individuals who shared his desire for freedom, equality, and a brighter future. Together, they would strive to bring about a change that would impact not only their lives but the destiny of humanity itself.

And so, with unwavering resolve, Hubris embraced the mission that lay before him. He was ready to face the challenges, to uncover the mysteries, and to stand up against the oppressive forces that sought to control their world. In this moment, he became more than just Hubris; he became a vital part of the journey that would determine the fate of Black Dots and the future of all living beings.

Reader Disclaimer: Understanding Bubba's Transformation into Hubris

To fully grasp Bubba's transformation into Hubris and the profound journey that follows, readers are encouraged to explore the pages of the book "Black Dots." This previous narrative provides the essential back-story, context, and pivotal moments that shape Hubris's character and his involvement with the Black Dots mission.

"Black Dots" reveals the circumstances that led Bubba to become Hubris, the challenges he faced, and the choices he made, which ultimately connected him with Eoan, Ken, Broad, and the larger mission to reclaim freedom and equality.

By immersing yourself in the world of "Black Dots," you will gain a deeper understanding of Hubris's motivations, his commitment to the cause, and the evolving narrative that continues in the subsequent chapters. This viewer disclaimer ensures that you embark on Bubba's journey with the foundation and insight necessary to fully appreciate the path he has chosen and the adventures that lie ahead.

Broad instructed everyone to stand in front of the slots on the massive computer. It was a complex machine with five slots, each equipped with its individual keyboard. As the group of five approached the computer, a new challenge presented itself – they needed to enter a password. Broad pondered the situation, desperately searching for the right combination. Tension filled the room, and even he seemed uncertain.

With the clock ticking down, Rithi suggested, "Don't worry, Broad. Let's pray to God for guidance." The room fell into a moment of quiet contemplation as they collectively sought divine intervention.

The computer recognized each member one by one and gathered their unique information. However, when all five dots occupied their respective slots, it prompted them for another challenge – rearranging the password in the correct order. This was the crucial Password Two.

With only a minute left, panic set in. The team frantically pondered the arrangement, struggling to decipher the correct sequence. Broad and Ken were on edge, knowing that time was running

out.

In a last-minute revelation, with just 20 seconds left, Broad saw the solution. He swiftly assigned each of the five individuals to their designated slots. Eoan stood in the first slot, Aplade in the second, Rithi in the third, Tyro in the fourth, and finally, Hubris in the fifth and last slot. The computer began to react, lights flashing and emitting gas that enveloped the area, obscuring their vision.

Then, with a deafening noise, the computer powered down and a brilliant green light illuminated the room. Confusion reigned as the team struggled to comprehend the situation. In that moment, Ken spoke up, his voice trembling with excitement, "We did it! Congratulations, everyone. Our mission is accomplished!" The significance of their achievement started to sink in, and a sense of accomplishment washed over them.

However, Hubris realized that his path was different from that of the Black Dots. He had to leave them to pursue his own journey. The Black Dots, now aware of the truth and with a heavy heart, felt compelled to give him a heartfelt send-off. As he departed, they watched him vanish into the horizon, wishing him well in his newfound purpose. The next chapters of their story would continue without him, but the impact of his presence would forever linger in their hearts.

Bubba, once again a seven-year-old boy, stood among his friends as they waved goodbye to Hubris, the remarkable individual who had joined them during their most critical mission. The wisdom of age had transformed him into a twenty-five-year-old man, but now, due to the insect's bite, he had reverted to his original form. Yet, the experiences he had gained, and the connections he had forged, would stay with him.

The Black Dots, still processing the significance of their achievement, turned their attention to the journey that lay ahead. The next chapters of Bubba's story is about to unfold, and he is ready to face whatever challenges and adventures awaited him.

CHAPTER THREE

THE STONE FISH'S SECRET

Bubba entered the ancient temple dedicated to the sea god. Its stone walls bore the marks of countless years, and the scent of saltwater clung to the air, invoking a sense of reverence. He gazed upon the central altar, which stood as a testament to the faith of fishermen who ventured into the unforgiving sea. At its heart lay a majestic idol of the sea god, a towering figure carved from the finest coral.

As Bubba approached, his eyes were drawn to the altar's base, where offerings had been placed by devout fishermen over the years. Among the shells, incense, and tokens was a small, intricately carved stone fish, a precious gift from his father, Morvane, before Bubba's unexpected departure on the rich man's boat.

Bubba felt a rush of emotions, his eyes welling with tears as he picked up the stone fish. It was a symbol of his father's love, a reminder that, despite their hardships, there was always a connection between them, as deep as the ocean itself. He clutched the stone tightly, vowing to return to his family and celebrate his next birthday together, with the gift of the carved fish held in both hands.

Amid the tranquil atmosphere of the temple, a strange insect appeared. It was unlike any Bubba had ever seen, with iridescent wings and a shimmering, translucent body. The insect landed gently on the altar, its multifaceted eyes locking onto Bubba with an otherworldly intelligence.

Intrigued by the insect's presence, Bubba extended a finger, allowing the delicate creature to perch upon it. He marvelled at its beauty and wondered if it held any significance within the temple. As the insect crawled across his palm, he felt a subtle sting, followed by a curious sensation that swept over him.

Unbeknownst to Bubba, this seemingly ordinary insect held extraordinary powers, and its bite had triggered an extraordinary transformation, sending ripples across the fabric of time and space, leading him toward a destiny intertwined with the mysteries of the sea, the legacy of his family, and the ongoing journey of the Black Dots.

Morvane had just finished his gruelling day at the docks, returning from a long and demanding journey at sea. His calloused hands and weathered face bore testimony to the hardships he endured as a fisherman, but his heart was as warm as ever. On this particular evening, his thoughts were focused on the promise he had made to his son, Bubba, a promise he was determined to fulfil this time.

As he walked toward the humble, weather-beaten cottage that he called home, Morvane felt a sense of anticipation welling up within him. Bubba had asked about his upcoming birthday, and Morvane intended to make it a day to remember. A cake, no matter how simple, and perhaps a small gift, would bring the joy of celebration to his son's life.

Upon reaching the cottage, Morvane opened the creaking wooden door, revealing the cozy interior. The flickering candlelight cast a warm and inviting glow. Nerissa, his wife, was busy preparing their modest dinner, her eyes reflecting the worry that had settled upon their lives due to their financial struggles.

Morvane approached her, his face breaking into a tired yet affectionate smile. "Nerissa," he began, "I've been thinking about Bubba's birthday, you know? Its tomorrow, and I've made a promise to him."

Nerissa turned from her tasks, her eyes meeting her husband's. She understood the promise Morvane was referring to, and the impossibility of fulfilling it in their current circumstances. "Morvane, you know how much I want to make Bubba's birthday special, but we barely have enough to make ends meet. Our financial situation..."

Morvane nodded, knowing the truth of her words all too well. Their life was a constant struggle, with barely enough money to cover the essentials. Every day was a battle against the unforgiving sea, and every night was marked by uncertainty. "I know, Nerissa," Morvane replied, his voice tinged with resignation. "I just wish I could give our boy the birthday he deserves. He's seen other children celebrate their special days, and I've let him down time and time again."

Nerissa reached out and took her husband's hands, her eyes filled with empathy and love. "Morvane, you're a good father. Bubba knows that. He'll understand that this year, like the others, we can't afford a big celebration."

Morvane's gaze turned toward the rough-hewn table, and he sighed. "I just wish there was something I could do to bring a smile to his face."

Little did Morvane know that his wish would set a chain of events into motion that would forever change the course of their lives. As the night enveloped the small cottage and the candles continued to flicker, hope mingled with uncertainty, casting long shadows on their journey ahead.

This year was different because, just before Morvane set off on a voyage, he visited an ancient temple nestled among the rugged cliffs by the sea. This temple, rumoured to be centuries old, held an aura of mystique that had intrigued him. It was dedicated to the sea god, believed to be the guardian of fishermen and sailors, and it was a place where many came to seek blessings and safety on their maritime journeys.

Inside the temple, Morvane had felt an unusual connection with the sea god. He observed the time-worn stone statues and the incense-laden air that clung to the temple's ancient walls. Among the worn stones, he discovered a small, unassuming rock, seemingly imbued with an energy that captivated his senses. He couldn't explain it, but he felt compelled to take it with him, sensing that it held a significance he couldn't quite grasp.

During his voyage, that small stone became a source of comfort and inspiration for Morvane. He'd carve the stone into a delicate fish shape during his hours of solitude on the sea. As he meticulously shaped and polished it, he imbued the fish with his hopes, dreams, and love for his son, Bubba. Morvane envisioned the fish as a symbol of protection, a guardian to watch over his son in his absence. On the morning of Bubba's birthday, Morvane returned home, carrying the hand-carved fish as his gift. As he presented it to Bubba, he explained its origin, sharing the story of the ancient temple and the connection he had felt with the sea god. The gift was more than just a beautifully crafted stone; it was a representation of Morvane's love, wishes for his son's safety, and his desire to instil in Bubba a deep respect for the sea.

Bubba was moved by his father's gesture and the story behind the fish. He accepted the gift with a sense of reverence and promised to keep it with him always, understanding that it was not just an object, but a symbol of his father's unwavering love and the mysterious connection they shared with the sea.

The stone fish became a cherished family heirloom, passed down through generations, carrying with it the love, hopes, and dreams of the fishermen in Morvane's lineage. Each year on Bubba's birthday, they would gather around the small, hand-carved fish and share stories of the sea, their father's adventures, and their own experiences on the water. It was a reminder of the unbreakable bond they had with the sea and with each other, a testament to the enduring power of a father's love for his son.

Bubba found himself sitting alone in the ancient temple once more at the age seventy four, where the sea air was heavy with history and whispered secrets. This time, he was not alone; a friendly dog had joined him, its presence seemingly just as mystifying as the temple itself.

As he gazed at the stone fish that had been in his family for generations, Bubba couldn't help but feel an uncanny connection to it. It had seen countless birthdays, heard tales of the sea, and witnessed the passage of time. There was something about the fish, something beyond its physical form, that drew him closer to it.

The temple seemed to come alive in a peculiar way. The air grew thick with anticipation, and the gentle hum of the sea in the background seemed to synchronize with the temple's vibrations. Bubba, perplexed yet curious, reached out and touched the stone fish. At that very moment, an eerie sensation rippled through him, as if he had awakened some ancient force.

The dog at his side remained calm, as if it, too, was aware of the temple's mysteries. It sat by Bubba's feet, watching him with intelligent eyes that held a glimmer of understanding. The dog's presence was both comforting and enigmatic.

As Bubba continued to study the stone fish, he noticed something unusual—a faint glimmer from within the temple walls. In the dim light, he discerned the source: an insect, unlike any he had ever seen before. It was a brilliant iridescent creature, with wings that seemed to reflect the colours of the sea. The insect hovered around the fish, seemingly drawn to it.

The air grew even heavier as Bubba's sense of wonder deepened. The stone fish, the mysterious insect, the dog, and the ancient temple seemed to converge in a harmonious yet cryptic dance. Bubba felt like he was on the cusp of uncovering an age-old secret, one that had been waiting for him, passed down through generations, encapsulated within the stone fish's enigmatic aura. As the iridescent insect continued its intricate ballet around the fish, Bubba couldn't shake the feeling that he had become part of a story that transcended time and space. It was a tale of connections, of an unbroken bond between his family and the sea, and the inexplicable force that linked them all in this sacred place.

The temple pulsated with a subdued energy, and the line between reality and the mystical began to blur. Bubba felt that he was at the precipice of an extraordinary revelation, one that would not only connect him with his family's heritage but also unveil the ancient wisdom that the sea and the temple held.

As Bubba gently placed the stone fish on the temple's ancient floor, he felt a sudden, inexplicable connection. It was as if the very essence of the temple was responding to his touch, and in an instant, the world around him transformed.

A brilliant flash of light engulfed the temple, blinding him momentarily. When he could see again, he realized that the dog was no longer at his side, and the mysterious insect had vanished. In their place, there was a profound stillness, and Bubba found himself sitting on the cool stone floor. But what astounded him the most was the change he felt within himself.

Bubba had returned to his seven-year-old self. His once-adult body had regressed to the innocence of childhood. Confusion mixed with amazement as he looked down at his small hands, his childlike legs, and his clothes, which now hung loosely on his tiny frame. He reached up to touch his face and found that it was smooth and unburdened by the marks of adolescence.

The temple's atmosphere seemed to resonate with an enigmatic force. Bubba was no longer just a visitor; he was now part of a living legend. The stone fish, which he had once believed to be a mere family heirloom, had revealed its secrets in the most extraordinary way. It was a conduit to a mystical transition, a guardian of ageless wisdom, and a bridge between the past and the future.

As Bubba contemplated this surreal transformation, a voice echoed softly in his mind, as if whispered by the very walls of the temple. The voice seemed to unravel the mysteries hidden within the stone fish. It told of an ancient sea god, the protector of those who ventured out to sea, and the keeper of the knowledge of the oceans.

The stone fish, a creation of the ancient civilization that had built the temple, had been forged from an otherworldly mineral that harnessed the energy of the sea. It was intended to preserve the knowledge and experiences of those who touched it, enabling them to transcend time itself.

Bubba, in his youthful form, had become the chosen vessel. The stone fish had recognized his unyielding connection to the sea, his family's enduring bond with the waters, and his yearning to understand the mysteries of the deep. The temple, acting as a conduit for the stone fish's power, had granted him a glimpse into the past and the key to unlock the future.

But with this gift came responsibility. Bubba now held the legacy of countless generations, the collective wisdom of sailors, and the secrets of the ocean. The sea god's ancient knowledge, stored within the stone fish, was meant to be shared with the world to safeguard the seas and the creatures that dwelled within them.

As Bubba sat there, the weight of this newfound understanding settled upon his young shoulders. He realized that he was chosen to carry forward the knowledge of the sea, to bridge the gap between the past and the future, and to be a guardian of the oceans. This moment in the temple had not only revealed his destiny but also unveiled the deep-rooted connection between his family, the stone fish, and the sacred waters they revered.

With a sense of purpose and reverence, young Bubba knew that his journey was far from over. He was now the keeper of the sea god's wisdom, and the stone fish was his guide to unlocking the secrets of the ocean's depths, understanding the mysteries of the world, and protecting the maritime legacy of his ancestors. The path ahead was filled with adventure, discovery, and the opportunity to make a profound difference in the world, guided by the wisdom of the stone fish and the enduring spirit of the sea.

CHAPTER FOUR

INTRUDERS FROM THE SKY

Seven-year-old Bubba sat cross-legged on the cool, worn stone floor of the ancient temple dedicated to the sea god. The dim light filtered through narrow windows, casting a pattern of shadows on the walls. He had come to this place with a purpose, but now, as he gazed at the serene, weathered statue of the sea god, he was overwhelmed by conflicting thoughts and emotions.

Bubba missed his parents terribly. The memories of their warm smiles, the comforting sound of their voices, and the safety of their home weighed heavily on his young heart. He felt a profound sense of homesickness that gnawed at him from the inside.

Tears welled up in his eyes as he remembered the day he had left his village, promising his parents that he would find a way to save them from the perilous situation that had gripped their community. He was determined to be their hero, but now, in this ancient temple, he was beginning to doubt himself.

Bubba's head was filled with a swirling vortex of thoughts, each one more confusing than the last. What could he, a small child, possibly do to change their fate? The weight of his responsibility was heavy, and it seemed impossible to bear.

As Bubba stared at the sea god's statue, a gentle breeze swept through the temple, carrying with it the scent of saltwater and the distant calls of seagulls. It was as if the sea god was trying to communicate with him, to offer some guidance in his moment of confusion.

Bubba took a deep breath, trying to steady his racing heart. He knew he couldn't give up, he had come this far, and he owed it to his parents and his village to continue. With renewed determination, he wiped away his tears and whispered a heartfelt prayer to the sea god, asking for strength, wisdom, and the courage to face the challenges that lay ahead.

With his prayer spoken, Bubba felt a sense of peace wash over him, and he realized that he might be a small child in a vast world, but his determination and the support of the sea god would guide him on his journey. He didn't have all the answers yet, but he was no longer clueless. He had found a spark of hope and purpose within the walls of the ancient temple, and he was ready to face whatever challenges awaited him on his path to becoming a hero.

Bubba's curiosity had always been one of his defining traits, and the mysterious vibrations he felt in the temple's walls only piqued his interest further. He decided to explore the temple more thoroughly, feeling a sense of purpose in this ancient place. As he ventured deeper into the temple's main chamber, his eyes were drawn upward to the ceiling, where he noticed a small slot shaped like two fish intertwined.

In one half of the slot, a stone fish was perfectly fitted, but the other half remained conspicuously empty. Bubba, clutching the stone fish he had found earlier, couldn't help but wonder if this was the key to some hidden secret or knowledge that the temple held. The pieces of the puzzle were slowly coming together in his young mind.

The slot in the shape of two fish was a mystery, a riddle waiting to be solved. He knew he needed to find a way to fit his stone fish into the empty half of the slot, but as a short, seven-year-old boy, he wasn't tall enough to reach it. Bubba looked around; searching for something to help him, and his eyes fell upon a weathered, wooden bench tucked in a corner of the chamber.

With determined steps, he dragged the bench beneath the slot. It was heavy and took some effort, but Bubba was not easily deterred.

He stood on the bench, his small hands trembling with anticipation, and tried to fit the stone fish into the vacant slot. As he did so, a faint click echoed through the chamber, and the walls seemed to vibrate once again, but this time with a purpose.

Suddenly, the temple was bathed in a soft, ethereal light that seemed to emanate from the stone fish. The sea god's statue, once shrouded in shadows, now glowed with an otherworldly radiance. Bubba's heart raced as he realized that he had uncovered a hidden secret within the temple, something that held great significance.

With the temple now illuminated, Bubba noticed an ancient mural on the wall that he hadn't seen before. It depicted the legend of a heroic young fisherman who, like him, had embarked on a quest to save his village from a great calamity. Bubba felt a deep connection to this story, and he realized that he was on the right path.

As Bubba continued to explore the temple, he knew that the stone fish and the riddle it had unlocked were just the beginning of his journey. With newfound determination, he set out to unravel the mysteries of the temple and gather the knowledge and strength he needed to fulfil his mission and become the hero he aspired to be.

Bubba stood in awe of the ancient mural, its vivid colours and intricate details telling the story of the heroic fisherman who had come before him. However, his sense of wonder was tinged with a feeling of unease as he noticed the two cameras discreetly nestled into the mural. One camera had just activated, its lens trained on him, while the other blinked, not yet fully active. These devices were unlike anything Bubba had ever seen in his young life. The concept of surveillance and being watched was entirely foreign to him. He couldn't help but feel a sense of intrusion and vulnerability, as though unseen eyes were scrutinizing his every move.

Bubba took a step back, his eyes darting from one camera to the other. He wondered who had placed these cameras here and why they were observing him. The sea god's temple, a place of reverence and mystery, had suddenly become a place of uncertainty and questions.

The camera that was activated seemed to follow Bubba's movements as he cautiously explored the chamber. He couldn't escape the feeling that someone, or something, was monitoring him. It was as if the ancient mural itself had come to life, and he was now a character in a story being observed by an unknown audience.

As he pondered the significance of the cameras, a realization dawned on him. Perhaps the cameras were not meant to be invasive or harmful. Instead, they might hold clues to the secrets of the temple, providing guidance or insights to those who dared to solve its mysteries.

With newfound strength of mind and a sense of purpose, Bubba decided to treat the cameras as tools to untie the temple's enigmatic past. He would continue his exploration, paying attention to the subtle cues and messages that the cameras might convey, in the hopes of finding answers to the questions that had led him to this sacred place.

With each step, the young hero grew more resolute, ready to face the unknown and embrace the challenges of his extraordinary journey, all the while being aware that he was under the watchful gaze of the ancient mural's cameras.

As Bubba stepped onto one of the stone tiles that appeared different from the others, he immediately noticed a strange sensation beneath his foot. The tile felt hollow, and the sound of his footsteps, a muted thud compared to the solid stones around it, confirmed his suspicion. He had stumbled upon something intriguing.

Kneeling down, Bubba examined the tile closely. He ran his small fingers over its surface, feeling the intricate carvings of thin lines and mysterious shapes etched into the stone. The symbols seemed to tell a story, a narrative hidden within the very foundation of the temple.

As his fingers traced the symbols, he noted that they were not mere decorations but a deliberate language or code. It was a language he had never seen before, yet he sensed that it held the key to unscrambling the temple's secrets.

Bubba's excitement and curiosity surged. He couldn't help but wonder if this coded message might be the next piece of the puzzle, a clue that would lead him closer to understanding the purpose of the temple and his own mission. He knew he needed to decipher this enigmatic script to continue his journey.

Carefully, he took out a piece of parchment and a piece of charcoal from his bag, using the stone tile as a makeshift desk. He began to copy the symbols, determined to decipher their meaning. Each stroke of the charcoal felt like progress, and with each symbol he transcribed, the path ahead seemed to grow clearer. The language of the temple was slowly revealing its secrets to him.

As Bubba worked on deciphering the symbols, he couldn't help but feel that he was on the brink of a significant discovery, one that might not only guide him in the temple but also hold the key to understanding the larger mysteries surrounding his quest and the ancient sea god's temple.

As Bubba diligently copied the ancient carvings onto his parchment, he couldn't shake the feeling that he wasn't alone in the temple. The soft scraping of the charcoal was joined by an eerie sound, a faint rustling coming from the other side of the wall. He turned his head, trying to locate the source of the noise.

Intrigued and somewhat apprehensive, Bubba followed the sound, which led him to a small, hidden door nestled near the corner of the main chamber. The door was old and weathered, its wood bearing the marks of countless years. It was secured with a heavy chain that, to his astonishment, appeared to be glowing with strange reflections and intricate patterns. The chain seemed to pulse with an otherworldly energy, drawing his attention like a moth to a flame.

Bubba realized that this peculiar door and its enigmatic chain held another layer of mystery within the temple. It was as though the temple was guiding him deeper into its secrets, using his curiosity as a beacon. The symbols he had copied from the stone tile suddenly felt even more significant, as if they were part of a larger puzzle that extended beyond the mural and into this hidden chamber.

He carefully examined the glowing patterns on the chain, trying to decipher their meaning. Were they some kind of protection or a warning? Bubba couldn't be sure, but he knew that to continue his journey and uncover the temple's secrets, he would have to find a way to unlock this mysterious door. With newfound resolve and a sense of purpose, Bubba turned his attention to the chain, his young mind racing with thoughts of how he might unravel this latest riddle and discover what lay beyond the door, which held the promise of even more answers and adventures.

As Bubba's small hand brushed the surface of the glowing chain, he expected to encounter resistance, but to his astonishment, the chain seemed to react to his touch. It emitted a faint, otherworldly chime, and then, like a serpent slithering into its hole, the chain retracted into the door's cover with a series of metallic clicks.

The door began to transform before his eyes, its rusted metal and aged wood becoming pristine and crystal clear. It morphed into a door made entirely of shimmering glass, the edges of which were outlined by intricate wooden frames that bore symbols and markings he had never seen before.

In the glass door, Bubba saw his own reflection staring back at him, but there was something uncanny about it. As he studied the reflection more closely, he realized that it wasn't just his own face. There, on the other side of the glass, stood another boy of similar age and appearance, mirroring his every movement.

A sense of awe and curiosity washed over Bubba as he contemplated the duality of the glass door. It was as if he were looking at a reflection of himself, but on the other side of reality. With a mix of trepidation and excitement, he wondered about the identity of the boy on the other side and what this extraordinary door might reveal.

Drawing a deep breath, Bubba decided to cross the threshold, his hand gently pushing against the glass surface. The moment his fingers made contact with the cool, clear door, a tingling sensation coursed through him, and he stepped into a world that seemed to exist in parallel to his own, where the mysteries of the temple and his quest were bound to unravel further.

As Bubba stepped through the glass door and into the parallel world, he was met with the warm greeting of the boy on the other side. The familiarity in the boy's eyes and the friendly smile on his face made it seem as if they had known each other for a long time. Yet, for Bubba, Tyro was a complete stranger.

Bubba couldn't help but feel a mixture of curiosity and confusion. His hand instinctively went to his pocket, retrieving the stone fish he had found earlier. To his amazement, Tyro, the boy on the other side, mirrored his actions,

revealing an identical stone fish.

Their mutual display of the stone fish seemed to be a symbol of recognition and connection, but it deepened the mystery for Bubba. How did Tyro have the same stone fish, and why did he seem to know Bubba so well?

They exchanged introductions, and Bubba learned that the boy's name was Tyro. Tyro's words and demeanour conveyed a sense of friendship and shared experiences, but Bubba remained puzzled. For him, Tyro was an enigma, a person from a world he had never known.

Tyro's eyes held a glimmer of understanding, as if he possessed knowledge about Bubba that was beyond Bubba's own understanding. It was as if Tyro had been waiting for his arrival, anticipating their meeting.

With a mixture of caution and curiosity, Bubba embarked on a conversation with Tyro, hoping to unravel the mysteries of this parallel world and the connection between them. There were questions to be answered and secrets to be uncovered, and the glass door had led him into a realm that held the promise of remarkable discoveries and adventures.

Bubba was struck by the uncanny resemblance between Tyro and the figure on the mural he had discovered in the temple. The likeness was so precise that it sent shivers down his spine. It was as though Tyro had stepped out of the very history of the temple itself.

With a sense of trust and curiosity growing within him, Bubba followed Tyro into a small, car-like chamber that resembled nothing he had ever seen before. The chamber exuded an otherworldly aura, filled with controls and displays that were beyond his comprehension.

Tyro, however, seemed right at home. He expertly navigated the controls and activated a camera within the main chamber of the temple. As the camera powered up, Bubba's sense of wonder was accompanied by a dawning realization. It was this technology, this chamber, and the camera that had allowed Tyro to bring the temple back to its original condition when he had first entered.

The temple, once again bathed in a serene and ancient glow, was restored to the state in which Bubba had first encountered it. It was as if time itself had been rewound to that initial moment. The experience left Bubba in awe of the powers at play in this world, where technology and mysticism intertwined in ways he could hardly fathom.

With a mix of gratitude and wonder, Bubba couldn't wait to explore the temple anew with Tyro by his side. The mysteries surrounding this ancient place and his unexpected companion only seemed to deepen. There was much to learn, much to uncover, and the journey ahead held the promise of answers that might reshape Bubba's understanding of the world and his place within it. Bubba marvelled at the incredible technology that Tyro possessed. It was a world-changing discovery that offered glimpses into the past and present, opening doors to a realm of knowledge and exploration he could hardly fathom.

As the holographic image of his parents celebrating his birthday continued to play out, he noticed the look of joy on their faces and the flickering candles on the cake. A deep sense of nostalgia and warmth filled Bubba's heart. He had missed this moment, and it was as though time had paused for him to relive it.

With tears glistening in his eyes, Bubba whispered, "Thank you, Tyro. This means the world to me. I can't believe I'd ever doubt your incredible technology." He was grateful for this unexpected connection to his past and the love his parents had shown him.

Tyro smiled warmly at Bubba, pleased to have given him this precious gift. "It's a small taste of what we can explore together, Bubba. The chamber holds vast knowledge and countless experiences, waiting for us to uncover. Your journey to become a hero just got a lot more exciting, don't you think?"

Bubba nodded, his mind spinning with the possibilities. "I feel like there's so much to learn, to discover, and to understand. This chamber is a treasure trove of knowledge and adventure. I can't wait to see where it leads us." Their friendship had already begun to unlock the secrets of the ancient temple, and the bond between Bubba and Tyro would prove to be a formidable force in their quest for heroism. As they stood before the incredible interface of the chamber, they were filled with anticipation, eager to continue their journey into the mysteries of the world and the extraordinary powers at their disposal.

As the holographic image of his parents celebrating his birthday played before him, Bubba couldn't hold back his tears. The joy on their faces, the flickering candles on the cake—it was a bittersweet moment that filled him with a deep sense of longing. Gratitude swelled in his heart for Tyro, who had given him this unexpected glimpse into the past.

Amid the background of the video, where his family celebrated, Bubba turned to Tyro. "Thank you so much, Tyro. I can't believe I ever doubted this amazing technology."

Tyro replied with a warm smile, "You're welcome, Bubba. This is just the beginning of what we can uncover together."

Bubba couldn't help but ask the question that had been on his mind ever since he first saw the cake in the video. "Tyro, why didn't my parents show me the cake when I was there? I thought our family was going through such tough times. I was planning to work to support my father."

Tyro nodded, understanding the confusion. "Your parents did intend to surprise you with that cake the day after your birthday, Bubba. They wanted to give you a special celebration. But something miraculous happened. When you left, you were filled with a deep desire to help your family. You went above and beyond to secure their well-being. And in the process, you found something extraordinary."

Bubba was puzzled by Tyro's words. "Something extraordinary? What do you mean?"

Tyro smiled knowingly and, with a few swift commands, adjusted the interface. On the screen, Bubba watched in astonishment as the live video feed from the chamber showcased a live stream from his family's home. In this real-time video, he saw his parents, Morvane and Nerissa, standing before a beautifully renovated home. The place had been upgraded and improved, and a joyous atmosphere filled the air. His parents were laughing and chatting with a younger version of Bubba, who was right there with them.

Bubba was taken aback, struggling to comprehend what he was seeing. "How is this possible? I was on a boat during that time. I wasn't with them."

Tyro explained, "Your unwavering determination and love for your family, Bubba, inadvertently created a unique opportunity. As you worked on the boat, your intentions and efforts resonated across time and space. It was as though another version of you appeared right beside your parents, and together, you improved their lives. Your hard work had a profound impact, even when you weren't physically present."

Bubba was deeply moved, tears welling up once again. The revelation that his love and dedication had touched his family, even from a distance, was both heart-warming and magical. As they continued to watch the live stream of Bubba's parents, joyous and thriving, Bubba couldn't help but feel a renewed sense of purpose. The chamber, Tyro, and the incredible technology at their disposal held the power to unveil the wonders of the world, and Bubba was determined to explore, learn, and make a difference in the lives of those he loved.

With Tyro as his guide and companion, Bubba was ready to face whatever mysteries and adventures lay ahead, understanding that the bonds of love and dedication could transcend time and space, weaving a tapestry of hope and wonder in the world.

Bubba turned to Tyro, his heart brimming with gratitude and curiosity. "Tyro, this is incredible. I never imagined that my efforts could impact my family in such a profound way, even when I was miles away. It's like a miracle."

Tyro nodded, his eyes reflecting the wonder of the moment. "It is a remarkable testament to the power of determination and love. Your actions, guided by your love for your family, had a ripple effect that transcended the boundaries of time

and space."

Bubba couldn't help but wonder, "Is this technology what the sea god's temple is all about? Is there more to discover, more mysteries to unravel?"

Tyro's response was thoughtful. "The temple is a place of incredible knowledge and power, but it's not just about technology. It's about understanding the interconnectedness of all things, about the forces that shape our world and our destinies. The temple is a vessel that allows us to explore the depths of this understanding."

Bubba felt a deep sense of purpose welling up within him. "I want to continue exploring, to learn and to make a difference in the world. There's so much I still don't understand, and I want to unlock the secrets of the temple."

Tyro's gaze held a sense of willpower. "I believe, together, we can uncover the temple's mysteries and harness its knowledge for the greater good. But, Bubba, our journey is just beginning. There are challenges and adventures awaiting us. Are you ready for what lies ahead?"

Bubba met Tyro's gaze with unwavering resolve. "I'm ready, Tyro. I want to be a hero, not just for my family, but for everyone who needs help. Let's embrace the unknown and continue this incredible journey."

With a shared sense of purpose and the mysteries of the temple beckoning, Bubba and Tyro were prepared to face whatever lay ahead. The chamber and the technology it held were their tools, but their determination and love would be their greatest assets on this extraordinary path. The story was far from over, and a new chapter was about to unfold.

CHAPTER FIVE

INTO THE BLUE UNKNOWN

The chamber-like device that Tyro had used to reveal Bubba's family celebration was, in fact, a remarkable underwater vessel. With their hearts filled with excitement and curiosity, Bubba and Tyro prepared to embark on an incredible journey into the deep ocean.

As they settled into the chamber's comfortable seats, Tyro initiated the vessel's systems. It hummed to life, and the clear glass walls that surrounded them began to change. The chamber transformed into a watertight, transparent submarine, allowing Bubba and Tyro to see the world beneath the waves.

Bubba watched in awe as the chamber descended beneath the ocean's surface. The water around them gradually transitioned from azure blue to a deeper, more mysterious shade. Schools of fish darted by, vibrant and diverse in color, and the vibrant coral reefs came into view.

Amidst the ever-changing underwater landscape, Bubba couldn't contain his wonder. "This is incredible, Tyro! I've never seen anything like this. The ocean is so full of life and beauty."

Tyro, with a smile on his face, agreed. "The ocean holds countless secrets and breathtaking sights, Bubba. But it also faces challenges and dangers. It's our responsibility to explore and protect this incredible ecosystem."

As they ventured further into the depths, the ocean began to reveal its secrets. Unique and exotic sea creatures swam by, from graceful sea turtles to elusive giant squids. The vibrant, alien-like landscape of the ocean floor came into view, with its mysterious underwater caves and deep-sea trenches.

Bubba's voice was filled with curiosity. "What are we looking for, Tyro? What mysteries does the ocean hold for us?"

Tyro glanced at him with a knowing look. "There are many discoveries awaiting us, Bubba. But our ultimate goal is to understand the interconnectedness of all life, just as the sea god's temple teaches. We must learn how to protect and preserve the delicate balance of this underwater world."

As the chamber continued its descent, taking them into the heart of the ocean's unknown depths, Bubba and Tyro were prepared to face the challenges and uncover the marvels that lay ahead. Their journey into the blue unknown was just beginning, and the wonders and responsibilities of the ocean world beckoned them to explore, learn, and make a difference in a world that was more mysterious and precious than they could have ever imagined.

As the submarine continued its descent into the deep ocean, the world outside transformed into an alien, mysterious realm filled with the wonders of marine life. Bubba couldn't contain his fascination, and his curiosity couldn't help but bubble up. "Tyro," he began, "I've been wondering... where you come from? What's your origin, your story?"

Tyro, always ready to share knowledge, glanced at Bubba with a knowing smile.

"Bubba, my origin is a tale that begins far beyond Earth. I come from a planet that, much like your own, has its share of challenges and discoveries. But let me show you the story of one individual who ventured to a distant planet in pursuit of knowledge and change."

With that, Tyro produced a cable-like device, and, in an instant, he connected it to the palm of Bubba. The world around them seemed to freeze, and Bubba found himself watching a breathtaking scene, one that unfolded on a planet distant from Earth.

Bubba was captivated by the visuals, as they transported him to a foreign planet filled with advanced technology and a quest for change. The story that played before him was that of Dr. Cletus, the alien scientist, who had embarked on a daring journey to Earth.

Bubba watched in awe as the story of Dr. Cletus, his invention, and his transformation unfolded before him. He saw the scientist's arrival on Earth, his fascination with the unity and compassion of humans, and his mission to bring

those values back to his own people.

It was a story of enlightenment and change, of crossing boundaries to discover a new way of life. As the story played out, Bubba felt a connection with Dr. Cletus's journey. The power of unity and compassion, the same values that Mr. Cletus had seen in the humans of Earth, resonated with Bubba.

The cable disconnected from Bubba's palm, and time resumed its course. Bubba was left with a newfound appreciation for the power of unity and the potential for change, not only on Earth but also across the universe.

With a sense of purpose burning within him, Bubba turned to Tyro. "Tyro, the story of Dr. Cletus is inspiring. It shows that even in the vastness of the universe, values like unity and compassion can create profound change. I want to be a part of that change, not just on Earth but wherever we go."

Tyro nodded in agreement. "Bubba, your enthusiasm and dedication are remarkable. Together, we'll explore the deep ocean, learn from its mysteries, and bring back the knowledge and values that can inspire change, just like Dr. Cletus did."

As their journey into the blue unknown continued, Bubba and Tyro were now united by a shared mission and a deeper understanding of the power of unity and compassion in the universe. They were ready to embrace the ocean's challenges and unveil its secrets, all while carrying the story of Dr. Cletus as a source of inspiration.

In the era before Mr. Cletus's remarkable journey to Earth, the planet of the aliens was a place of advanced technology and scientific progress. Their society was built on the foundations of knowledge, with scientists and an inventor pushing the boundaries of what was possible. Among them, Mr. Cletus stood out as a brilliant and innovative scientist.

The planet, though technologically advanced, faced a significant challenge. Despite their scientific achievements, the society was characterized by a lack of unity and shared purpose. The inhabitants of the planet had become increasingly isolated and focused on individual pursuits. The values of compassion and cooperation had taken a backseat to technological progress.

Mr. Cletus, however, was different. He was deeply concerned about the growing disconnect among his people. While he was celebrated for his inventions and scientific breakthroughs, he was determined to use his knowledge to bridge the divide and restore unity to their society.

One day, he had a vision – the invention of the "Universal Scamodification" machine. His vision was not just to determine the gender of unborn babies but to use the machine's remarkable capabilities to read and modify the minds of their young. He believed that by instilling values of cooperation, compassion, and the greater good in the new generation, they could rebuild a society where technology and humanity went hand in hand.

But there was one significant problem. His fellow inhabitants were sceptical. They were accustomed to the pursuit of individual success, and they found it hard to believe that such a machine could instil values of unity. Mr. Cletus knew that people often required proof to embrace new ideas, and the machine's potential was met with disbelief.

He understood that he needed real-world evidence of the machine's effectiveness. He decided to take a bold step and journey into the unknown. He set off on an expedition to find a society where unity and compassion thrived. That's when he discovered Earth.

During his time on Earth, Mr. Cletus was profoundly impacted by the humans he encountered. He observed their ability to come together in times of need, to show compassion for one another, and to unite for the greater good. The experience transformed his perspective, not only as a scientist but as a fellow being in the universe.

Upon his return to his home planet, he brought back the blood samples from Earth, a physical reminder of the humans‘ potential for unity. But more importantly, he brought back a vision of change. He hoped to inspire his own people to embrace the values he had witnessed on Earth and to unite their technological advancements with the humanity he had found on that distant planet.

Deep beneath the ocean, Bubba and Tyro steered their submersible into an enchanting world. It was a cave that shimmered with an otherworldly light, thanks to special sea plants that glowed in shades of blue and green. The cave's walls sparkled with these radiant colours, creating an otherworldly, almost mystical ambiance.

This place was a wonder of nature, and it was teeming with unique, glowing sea creatures. Some of them were delicate and seemed almost transparent, moving gracefully like ethereal dancers through the water. Others, however, were more protective of their territory and displayed fierce, glowing patterns to communicate and ward off intruders.

As Bubba and Tyro ventured further into this unfamiliar environment, they encountered a world that was unlike anything they had ever seen before. Their advanced equipment allowed them to gather information about the creatures living in the cave. They observed their behaviours, the beautiful patterns of bioluminescence they displayed, and how they interacted with one another in the delicate ecosystem.

But their presence did not go unnoticed by the territorial creatures of the cave. These creatures, with sharp, glowing appendages, approached the submersible cautiously, curiously circling around it while making their territorial intentions clear.

Bubba and Tyro had to be careful and navigate their submersible with skill to avoid upsetting these creatures. They understood the importance of respecting the delicate balance of life in this unique underwater world. As they ventured deeper into this world of glowing wonders, Bubba and Tyro were amazed to discover that even in the darkest corners of the ocean, life could thrive and inspire awe. Their journey through this luminescent cave showcased the ocean's incredible ability to create breathtaking beauty and mystery. The challenges they faced only deepened their respect for the astonishing wonders hidden beneath the waves.

As Bubba and Tyro descended deeper into the trench, the pressure from the surrounding water continued to build, and the darkness grew more intense. Their high-tech chamber provided the only source of light in this strange, underwater world, casting eerie shadows all around.

Bubba, the oceanographer, was amazed by the unusual sea life they encountered. Giant, see-through creatures with shimmering scales glided past their chamber, their big, round eyes fixed on the unfamiliar visitors. Tyro, the engineer, was impressed by their chamber's strength, which held up well under the immense pressure of the deep sea.

But not all the creatures they met were friendly. Some, with sharp teeth and unfriendly eyes, tried to attack their chamber, mistaking it for food. Bubba and Tyro had to act quickly and use the chamber's defence system. It emitted a high-pitched sound that scared away the aggressive

creatures.

Their journey through the trench was about both surviving and learning. Bubba and Tyro used their advanced technology to gather data about these mysterious creatures while being careful not to disrupt the balance of this hidden world. They felt like humble guests in a place that had been hidden from humanity for a very long time. As they continued to explore deeper into the abyss, they stayed on high alert. They knew that around each corner of the trench, more enigmatic creatures could be waiting – some curious, others unfriendly. The adventure was far from over, and the mysteries of the deep sea were still waiting to be uncovered.

With each chapter of their oceanic exploration, Bubba and Tyro continued to learn, adapt, and gain a deeper appreciation for the ocean's incredible mysteries. This particular chapter left them in awe of the ocean's remarkable ability to nurture life even in the most unexpected and enchanting places. As the submarine glided through the mysterious depths of the ocean, Bubba couldn't help but feel a mixture of excitement and apprehension. The inky darkness outside was punctuated by the soft glow of bioluminescent creatures, creating an otherworldly ambiance within the submersible.

Bubba, his curiosity getting the better of him, turned to Tyro and asked, "You know, Tyro, this whole situation is quite bizarre. I mean, who leaves a submarine in a temple for years and then tells someone to pick it up without any idea of where we're heading? Do you have any hunch as to what's going on?"

Tyro scratched his head and replied with an uncertain tone, "Bubba, I wish I had more answers, but all I know is what I've been told. This submarine has its own navigation system, and I've been instructed to wait for you in that temple. Beyond that, it's a mystery. But sometimes, mysteries can lead to great adventures, don't you think?"

Bubba chuckled, his adventurous spirit rekindled. "You've got a point there, Tyro. It's not every day one finds them in a submarine in the middle of the ocean with no clear destination. I guess we're about to embark on one heck of an adventure. So, tell me, what do you do while you're waiting here in the temple for years? That can't be easy."

Tyro smiled, his eyes reflecting the wisdom of someone who had spent a long time in solitude. "Well, Bubba, I've spent my time studying the temple's ancient inscriptions and meditating. There's an aura of tranquillity and mystery about this place that's quite captivating. And, of course, I've been eagerly waiting for your arrival, which brings its own excitement."

As the submarine continued its descent into the abyss, Bubba and Tyro settled into a comfortable silence, occasionally exchanging thoughts about the beauty and mysteries of the deep-sea world surrounding them. The bioluminescent creatures outside danced like ethereal fireflies and the submarine's soft hum provided a soothing backdrop to their conversation.

Little did they know that their journey into the unknown had only just begun, and the secrets of the submarine, the temple, and the ocean's depths were waiting to be unravelled?

As their journey continued, Bubba and Tyro took a break to have their food supplements. The compact, high-tech pouches contained all the nutrients they needed for their undersea adventure. Bubba unscrewed the cap on his pouch and took a sip, making a face at the slightly synthetic taste.

Tyro, his pouch in hand, grinned and said, "Not the most gourmet meal, I admit, but it'll keep us going. Plus, it's an essential part of our mission."

Bubba nodded and, as he took another sip, his gaze fell on a peculiar crystal-like object on the tabletop. It was translucent and emitted a soft, pulsating glow, casting intricate patterns on the submarine's interior.

Curiosity got the best of him, and he reached out to pick up the crystal. As he held it in his hand, a peculiar warmth and sense of purpose washed over him. He turned to Tyro, excitement and intrigue in his eyes, and said, "Tyro, take a look at this. I found this crystal on the table, and there's something about it... it feels important, like it's trying to tell us something."

Tyro examined the crystal, his eyes widening as he recognized its significance. "Bubba, this is no ordinary crystal. It's an ancient artefact known as the 'Ocean's Heart.' Legend has it that the Heart possesses incredible powers and is said to guide those on a unique and important mission. It's been missing for centuries. This is remarkable!"

Bubba's heart raced with a mixture of awe and anticipation. "So, you mean to tell me that this crystal has something to do with our mission and this submarine?"

Tyro nodded gravely. "It seems that way, Bubba. The fact that you found it now, on this journey, is no coincidence. The Ocean's Heart has a way of choosing those it deems worthy for a mission of utmost importance. We need to decipher its message and follow its guidance. I believe it's the key to unlocking the mysteries that lie ahead."

With the Ocean's Heart in his pocket, Bubba and Tyro returned to their seats. Their excitement was palpable, and the submarine's navigation system seemed to respond to the presence of the ancient artefact. As the submersible continued its descent, the sense of purpose and the weight of their impending mission grew stronger. It was clear that their adventure was taking an unexpected and extraordinary turn, and the mysteries of the deep ocean were ready to reveal their secrets.

As the submarine glided through the dark depths of the ocean, the conversation between Bubba and Tyro turned to the mysteries of the universe, adding an intellectual layer to their journey.

Bubba, peering out into the vast expanse of the ocean beyond the submarine's thick porthole, mused, "You know, Tyro, this underwater world is like another universe, so different from the one we know up on the surface. It makes you wonder about the universe beyond our world, doesn't it?"

Tyro, always up for a thoughtful discussion, nodded. "Indeed, Bubba. The ocean depths are a reminder of how much of our planet remains unexplored, but they also remind me of the vastness of the universe beyond. The cosmos is a boundless expanse, and we've only scratched the surface of its secrets." Bubba continued, "I heard about this theory once, that there might be other intelligent life out there, in galaxies far, far away. Can you imagine what it would be like to make contact with extraterrestrial beings? That would be mind-blowing."

Tyro chuckled, "It would be a monumental discovery, for sure. Just think of the knowledge and perspectives they might bring. It's one of the most exciting possibilities in the realm of science fiction and science fact."

Their conversation took them to the concept of time and space, and Bubba pondered, "Time travel, too, is a fascinating idea. What if we could travel back in time and see historical events unfold, or maybe glimpse into the future? The possibilities are endless."

Tyro, intrigued by Bubba's curiosity, responded, "Time is a peculiar dimension, and while we've made great strides in understanding it, there's still so much we don't know. The fabric of time and space holds countless riddles that continue to captivate the minds of scientists and dreamers alike." Their conversation meandered through topics like black holes, the potential for parallel universes, and the concept of a multiversity. The darkness outside the submarine seemed to reflect the vastness of the universe, prompting a sense of humility and wonder in both Bubba and Tyro.

As they contemplated the mysteries of the universe, they couldn't help but feel that their current journey, guided by the enigmatic Ocean's Heart, was just a small part of a much grander cosmic narrative waiting to be unravelled. As Bubba and Tyro delved deeper into their conversation about the universe, Tyro, who was, in fact, an alien from an unknown planet, smiled to himself but maintained his human form and continued to act as if he was as curious as Bubba.

When Bubba mentioned the possibility of contact with extraterrestrial beings, Tyro's thoughts wandered to his home planet and the base hidden in the depths of the ocean. He knew that he was taking Bubba to a world unknown to humans, where Tyro's fellow aliens had established their base with the intention of studying Earth's oceans and fostering a peaceful connection with humanity. Tyro's mission was to bridge the gap between his people and the people of Earth.

As Bubba excitedly contemplated the concept of time travel, Tyro realized that the secrets of his advanced alien technology could soon be revealed to his new human companion. However, Tyro had a genuine intention behind this. He believed that by sharing his knowledge, he could help advance Earth's understanding of the universe and promote cooperation between the two species.

Their conversation continued, and Tyro shared his thoughts on black holes, parallel universes, and the multiversity, all while maintaining his human façade. He was well aware that the secrets of the ocean's depths, where his people had established their base, were connected to these mysterious concepts.

Unbeknownst to Bubba, Tyro's mission was not just about bringing him to the hidden underwater world of the aliens. It was about fostering a deeper understanding between their species, transcending the boundaries of Earth's surface and the far reaches of the universe. As the submarine descended further into the ocean's abyss, Tyro's hidden agenda remained concealed behind his friendly demeanour, leaving Bubba to wonder about the enigmatic secrets of the deep and the universe they were about to uncover together.

CHAPTER SIX

INTERMISSION

Amidst the turmoil of Cletus's ongoing mission to safeguard Earth from the alien threat, a pause emerges. This intermission marks a shift in perspective, a moment of contemplation, as the narrative embarks on a new path.

As the story momentarily recedes into the shadows, a fresh angle is about to be revealed. The journey takes an unexpected turn, unveiling hidden secrets and unexpected allies. The battle for Earth's survival enters a new phase, and Cletus faces challenges that will redefine his role as the planet's guardian.

In this intermission, take a deep breath, for the story is about to leap into uncharted territory, a world of intrigue, alliances, and uncharted frontiers.

Prepare to dive into the next chapter, where the enemy within takes a whole new form, and the stakes are higher than ever.

CHAPTER SEVEN

ENEMY WITHIN: EARTH'S SECRETS

As the story continued, the dire situation unfolded. Mr. Cletus, imprisoned by Dr. Scorch, had made vital modifications to his invention, the "Universal Scamodification Device" (USD Machine), just before his capture. These modifications were connected to the events on Earth and had a profound impact on the unfolding narrative.

Dr. Scorch, in a bid to control the human population and secure the future of the alien race on Earth, attempted to misuse the USD Machine. His sinister plan involved manipulating the minds of pregnant women on Earth. The device had the capability to influence the development of the next generation of humans, ensuring their loyalty to the alien invaders.

However, unknown to Dr. Scorch, Mr. Cletus had set a clever safeguard in place. He had programmed the machine with a unique security feature. The password to unlock the device was a sequence of five dots, and it was encoded with the condition that only a specific group of individuals coming together could unlock it.

Cletus had chosen this method to ensure that the machine could not be misused for nefarious purposes. The five individuals, who could trigger the machine, needed to have a particular set of characteristics or marks below their necks, as determined by Cletus's modifications.

As the story unfolded further, Eoan, one of the key characters, learned about these modifications from Broad. Eoan was tasked with finding the other four individuals who possessed the unique markings and bringing them together to unlock the USD Machine.

Broad, a character who had been instrumental in providing this crucial information, emphasized the urgency of the task. He stressed that they had only 23 days left to gather the group, and if they failed, catastrophic consequences awaited them. The survival of humanity depended on their success in gathering this group of five individuals

before the looming deadline.

Eoan's determination and sense of responsibility were kindled by Broad's words, and he set off on a mission to locate the other individuals who could activate the USD Machine. A sense of urgency and purpose now drove him as he understood the gravity of the situation.

This turn of events marked a critical juncture in the story, where the quest to gather the five individuals and prevent the impending disaster became the central focus. Eoan's journey to find and unite the members of this group, along with the unique communication network established by Broad using rats, played a pivotal role in the unfolding drama.

As the narrative continued, the suspense and anticipation grew, setting the stage for the race against time and the battle for the survival of humanity on Earth.

Dr. Scorch sat in his grandiose chamber, which was filled with alien artefacts and advanced technology. Mr. Cletus, now imprisoned, was brought before him, his posture exuding resilience. Scorch's eyes glinted with an unsettling determination.

Scorch: (smirking) "Cletus, you've always been the inquisitive one, haven't you? Exploring new frontiers, inventing these fascinating contraptions. It's a shame, really, that you turned your back on your own kind."

Cletus: (defiant) "I turned my back on destruction, Scorch. This isn't the way. Earth is a marvel, a planet teeming with life, and humans... they're an incredible species. They deserve to thrive."

Scorch: (grinning) "You've grown sentimental, Cletus. Sentiment has no place in our mission. Earth is just another resource, another piece of the puzzle. We must ensure our people's dominance, and that means harnessing the power of this planet."

Cletus: (determined) "I won't be part of this. You may have captured me, but you won't break my resolve. I've made sure of that." Scorch's brow furrowed with suspicion. He leaned closer to Cletus.

Scorch: "What are you talking about? What have you done?"

Cletus's eyes gleamed with a spark of cunning.

Cletus: "I've modified the USD Machine, Scorch. I've hidden the data about Earth, and only a group of five individuals with specific markings can access it."

Scorch: (angered) "You fool! You think your petty safeguards will stop me?"

Cletus: (smiling) "It's not about stopping you, Scorch. It's about ensuring Earth's secrets remain protected. You won't be able to control its destiny as long as those who truly value it can stand in your way."

Scorch seethed with frustration but knew that Cletus had outsmarted him. The battle for control over Earth had taken an unexpected turn, and the fate of the planet now hinged on the gathering of those with the unique markings, as Cletus had planned.

Dr. Scorch, his face contorted with anger and determination, had Cletus incapacitated. He didn't just want to silence him; he wanted to ensure there was no chance of Cletus interfering with his plans ever again.

With a wave of his hand, Scorch activated a series of advanced alien weapons that emitted a shimmering energy field. These weapons were designed to manipulate the very essence of a being's soul.

Scorch: (with an ominous tone) "Cletus, you've become an obstacle to our rightful control over Earth. I won't allow your defiance to persist."

Cletus, now unable to move or speak, watched in helpless horror as the energy field surrounded him, gradually enveloping his form. His once defiant eyes filled with fear as the process continued.

Scorch's underlings quickly moved into action, transferring Cletus to a specialized containment chamber, a transparent tank filled with an eerie, semi-translucent soil. The tank was designed to restrict any attempts at escape or communication with the outside world. Scorch: (addressing his followers) "Remember, we cannot allow anyone or anything to stand in our way. This is about the future of our kind and our dominance over Earth. If anyone opposes our mission, eliminate them."

Scorch's announcement sent shockwaves through his alien forces. They were now under strict orders to eliminate any opposition, no matter who it was.

As the story unfolded, Scorch's grip on power tightened, and the once-secretive mission to control Earth became increasingly ruthless. The fate of Earth and its inhabitants hung in the balance, and a sense of urgency permeated the narrative as Scorch's ruthless regime moved forward with its dangerous plans.

As Dr. Scorch stood on the precipice of realizing his dream of controlling Earth, a momentous shift occurred. He prepared to make his grand entrance, expecting to find Earth ripe for the taking, but what he encountered was beyond his wildest imagination.

To his astonishment, humans had not only returned to their normal state but had regained their wisdom and unity, akin to their ancestors. This transformation was a collective effort, a testament to the resilience of the human spirit. Throughout the world, there was a deep sense of gratitude as every individual celebrated their regained freedom. The group comprising Broad, Ken, Eoan, Rithi, Aplade, Tyro, and Hubris revelled in their success. They had not only secured their own freedom but had also saved the entire planet from Dr. Scorch's malevolent plans.

One of Scorch's assistants, aware of the monumental shift in humanity's favour, delivered the shocking news to his overlord.

Assistant: (with trepidation) "It's nearly impossible to combat the humans now. They've not only regained their technological prowess but have found unity among themselves."

Dr. Scorch, although taken aback, refused to accept defeat. His relentless ambition drove him to continue his plans, even if it meant resorting to insidious methods.

Scorch: (resolute) "It's not over yet. I've sowed the seeds of negativity in their minds. While they may appear united and good now, those dark

impulses will resurface from time to time."

To showcase his point, Scorch revealed an unusual device, the 'embryonic analyzer.' This machine had two columns, one in green and the other in red. The green column filled with each good deed a human did, while the red filled with each bad deed.

Scorch: "They may do good things, but they're still plagued by their negative tendencies. If the red reaches its limit, human unity will crumble, and their existence will be in peril."

With this foreboding declaration, the battle for Earth's destiny continued, and the line between victory and defeat remained perilously thin. The story's conclusion was far from certain, and the fate of humanity rested on a knife's edge.

Amidst the high-stakes battle between Dr. Scorch and the resolute humans, Mr. Cletus had a secret weapon of his own. It was an invention that allowed him to transmit his thoughts, ideas, and critical data as intricate patterns and frequencies. This technology was his last hope to protect the invaluable information about Earth's secrets, as Scorch had taken possession of his USD Machine.

However, there was a critical challenge - only the machine Scorch now controlled could decode these intricate patterns. It was a high-stakes cat-and-mouse game between the two former allies, with the future of Earth hanging in the balance.

Cletus's loyal friends, who had managed to escape from Scorch's clutches, embarked on a daring journey of their own. With the ability to breathe underwater, they plunged into the depths of the ocean, far from Scorch's menacing base. There, in the mysterious abyss, they worked tirelessly to establish a hidden alien base.

This underwater sanctuary, concealed in the darkest reaches of the ocean, would serve as a safe haven for those who opposed Scorch's malevolent designs. The base was equipped with advanced technology and guarded secrets that would ultimately help in the battle against Scorch's tyranny.

Meanwhile, Bubba and Tyro, in pursuit of their own mission, descended deep into the ocean. Unbeknownst to them, they were on a journey that would bring them to the alien base, a sanctuary of knowledge and hope hidden beneath the waves.

Their journey was not just a physical one; it was a voyage into the heart of the Earth's mysteries. The ocean depths held secrets of their own, and the deep-sea world was a realm of wonder, shrouded in mystique. Bubba and Tyro's quest would lead them to revelations about Earth's hidden history and its extraordinary defenders. As they ventured deeper into the abyss, they were unknowingly drawn towards the alien base, where the forces of good were gathering in preparation for a final stand against Dr. Scorch. The stage was set for a grand showdown beneath the waves, where the fate of Earth would be decided once and for all.

In the unfolding story, an intriguing and critical detail emerged: the stark contrast in lifespan between humans and aliens. This unique characteristic would become a pivotal factor in the narrative, creating a significant gap in age and experience between the two species. For humans, life on Earth was brief and fleeting, with an average lifespan of about 70 to 100 years. A human could live a century at best, and their lives were marked by the swift passage of time.

In stark contrast, the aliens possessed the extraordinary gift of longevity. A mere 10-year-old alien could be the equivalent of a 100-year-old human. This stark disparity in lifespan created profound differences in perspective and experience. Aliens observed the world with centuries of accumulated wisdom, while humans experienced life with the urgency of a fleeting moment.

This divergence in the perception of time and the value of each moment would play a significant role in the unfolding events. The age-old wisdom of the aliens, tempered by centuries of experience, would be pitted against the vibrancy and resilience of humanity, with their determination to safeguard their world.

The story would continue to explore the consequences of this age gap, examining how it influenced decisions, perspectives, and the ability to adapt to the ever-changing challenges that lay ahead. The juxtaposition of human transience and alien longevity would add depth and complexity to the narrative, shedding light on the contrasting strengths and vulnerabilities of the two species.

CHAPTER EIGHT

LIGHTS IN THE DEEP

As the submersible glided through the silent depths of the ocean, Bubba couldn't help but notice a mesmerizing sight in the distance. He tapped Tyro's shoulder and pointed towards the ethereal glow of neon colours that danced amid the darkness.

"Tyro, what is that beautiful place over there?" Bubba asked, his voice filled with wonder.

Tyro peered through the submersible's window, following Bubba's outstretched finger to the neon-lit spectacle. A knowing smile played on his lips. "That, my friend, is the Alien Base. It's not like any other place on Earth."

Bubba's eyes widened as Tyro explained. "You see, the aliens can breathe underwater just as easily as on land. They've created a massive air bubble beneath a colossal rock structure. This base gives them a unique advantage, allowing them to harness the resources of both the ocean and the land."

As they drew closer to the base, the scale of the operation became evident. The rock formation seemed almost like a natural island, camouflaging the advanced technology that lay hidden beneath. The neon lights weren't just for aesthetics; they served as a beacon to mark the location of this extraordinary underwater sanctuary.

Tyro continued, "This is the one place on Earth that could potentially stand against Dr. Scorch and any war that might arise between humans and aliens. The fusion of land and sea resources makes it a formidable stronghold."

Bubba nodded, realizing the strategic significance of the Alien Base. As they approached the entrance, he couldn't help but feel a mix of excitement and trepidation. What secrets and challenges awaited them in this enigmatic place?

The submersible descended into the air bubble, and they disembarked, greeted by alien creatures going about their business. The surreal blend of aquatic and terrestrial life was a testament to the ingenuity of these beings. Bubba and Tyro were about to embark on a journey that would not only uncover the mysteries of the Alien Base but also hold the key to humanity's future.

With each step they took into this remarkable underwater world, Bubba and Tyro felt the weight of their mission and the responsibility that came with it. The fate of Earth and its inhabitants now rested on their shoulders, as they delved deeper into the lights in the deep.

Inside the Alien Base, Bubba and Tyro disembarked from their submersible and were immediately surrounded by strange, alien-like creatures. The creatures had an air of familiarity about them, which puzzled Bubba. He had never been to this place before, so how did they seem to know him?

As Bubba observed the creatures more closely, he noticed some peculiar displays on the walls. These displays showed images of his mother, Nerissa, in a distant location, her current health status, and even what seemed to be live footage of her. In one display, he saw his father, along with other relatives, playing with a younger version of himself. It was as if they had been spying on him and his family for a long time.

Bubba couldn't believe his eyes. "How is this possible?" he muttered, feeling a surge of shock and confusion. He turned to Tyro, who had a serious expression on his face.

Tyro motioned for Bubba to follow as the alien creatures led them deeper into a cave-like structure within the base. Bubba had a million questions racing through his mind, but he couldn't voice a single one. The surreal nature of the situation left him dumbfounded.

As they entered the cave, the walls seemed to come alive with holographic projections, displaying the history of their interactions with Bubba's family over the years. The aliens had been monitoring and studying Bubba and his family for generations, and they had a deep understanding of human behaviour and biology.

Bubba's shock began to transform into a mixture of curiosity and apprehension. What was the purpose of this surveillance? Why were they so interested in his family, and what did they want from him now? With each step deeper into the alien base, the mysteries and questions grew, and Bubba was determined to find answers.

Bubba watched the holographic display, completely engrossed in the captivating story unfolding before him. The projection told the tale of a space traveller, Mr. Cletus, who had crash-landed on a new planet, Earth. As he stepped out of his spaceship and touched the alien planet's surface, a sense of wonder and excitement filled him.

The display vividly depicted Mr. Cletus's experience of Earth's gravity, his fascination with the unknown world, and his initial encounters with the planet's inhabitants. Bubba couldn't help but feel a sense of connection to this stranger's journey, even though it took place in the distant past.

As the hologram continued, Bubba witnessed Mr. Cletus observing Earth's creatures, including humans, from a distance. The display showed Mr. Cletus's mix of curiosity and trepidation as he hid behind a tree, keen to learn more about these

human beings.

Bubba's curiosity grew as he continued to watch the holographic story. Something in the back of his mind felt oddly familiar, but he couldn't quite place it. Little did he know that the roots of this connection ran much deeper than he could have imagined.

The hologram then detailed Mr. Cletus's attempts to collect samples from human bodies for his experiments. What Bubba didn't yet know was that the very first human sample ever collected had been that of his grandparents. Mr. Cletus had taken a keen interest in Bubba's family, and he had continued to monitor them for almost 30 Earth years, which amounted to only a few months for

Mr. Cletus and his fellow friends.

Unbeknownst to Bubba, Tyro, who had just moments ago left to tend to an urgent matter, was the son of Mr. Cletus. He had taken on the task of watching over Bubba and his family, ensuring that they remained safe and healthy. Their connection with humanity ran deep. As Bubba observed the holographic story, a strange alien creature approached him. The creature looked remarkably like Tyro, yet it was different enough to evade recognition. It spoke casually to Bubba, who couldn't discern its true identity.

Only after a few moments did the realization dawn on Bubba, and he stared in astonishment. "Tyro? Is that really you?" he asked, his eyes wide with amazement.

Tyro, in his alien form, nodded. "Yes, Bubba. I can transform myself into any form I choose. It's part of our abilities."

Bubba was astounded by the revelation. The intricate web of connections and the deep history between the aliens and his family left him in awe. The mysteries surrounding this place, his own heritage, and the role he was meant to play in these unfolding events had grown even more complex and intriguing.

As Bubba walked through the Alien Base, guided by Tyro, his amazement continued to grow. The base was a hub of activity, with humans and aliens working together in harmony. It was here that Earth's inhabitants were receiving training and knowledge from their extraterrestrial allies to advance and protect the planet.

Bubba couldn't believe what he was seeing. The humans in the base were undergoing various forms of training, learning from their alien counterparts. The scenes were a testament to the collective effort to safeguard Earth. Not only were humans being prepared, but even sea creatures, from the tiniest to the largest, were receiving instruction.

As Bubba observed a group of humans collaborating with dolphins, he couldn't help but approach them. The dolphins seemed to understand the human gestures and commands, working together in perfect harmony. Bubba struck up a conversation with one of the humans involved in this unique training program.

"Wow," Bubba exclaimed, "this is incredible! I never imagined that we could communicate with dolphins like this. How does it work?"

The human, a marine biologist named Sarah, smiled and replied, "It's a blend of technology and the aliens' understanding of marine life. We're using devices that help translate our signals into something dolphins can understand. With their intelligence and cooperation, we're making amazing progress in bridging the gap between our species."

Bubba nodded in awe. It was evident that this collaboration was not only beneficial for Earth's defence but also for fostering a deeper connection between humans and the creatures they shared the planet with.

As they continued their tour, Bubba couldn't help but feel a profound sense of hope and optimism. The base was a testament to the power of cooperation and knowledge-sharing, and the work being done here was a beacon of progress and preparation for the future.

Bubba turned to Tyro, who had been silently observing the scene. "This is amazing, Tyro. But why did you bring me here? What's my role in all of this?"

Tyro regarded Bubba with a knowing look. "We brought you here, Bubba, because you're a bridge between our two worlds. Your unique connection with humanity and your intelligence make you a vital part of our efforts to protect Earth. There's a role only you can play, and it's time we start preparing you for it."

Bubba's eyes widened as he approached a group of humans who were engaged in training magnificent water dragons and whales. One of the trainers, a woman with a warm and kind demeanour, noticed Bubba's curiosity and welcomed him with a smile. Her name was Dr. Olivia Finch, a marine biologist dedicated to understanding the complex relationship between humans and these majestic sea creatures.

Bubba couldn't contain his wonder and enthusiasm. "Dr. Finch, this is astonishing! I've never seen humans and sea creatures working together like this. How did you end up here in this remarkable place?"

Dr. Finch's eyes sparkled as she shared her story. "It's quite a journey, Bubba. It all started when Dr. Scorch initiated the Universal Scamodification Device. Many people, including me, were affected by it. But some of us, we managed to find

a way to resist its full effects."

Bubba furrowed his brow. "Resist? How?"

Dr. Finch leaned in, her voice filled with determination. "We discovered that by embracing the knowledge and assistance of our alien friends, we could build up our resistance to the Scamodification Device. They provided us with advanced techniques and treatments to counter its effects."

Bubba's curiosity deepened. "So, that's why you're here. You've found a way to protect yourselves from Dr. Scorch's devices."

Dr. Finch nodded. "Exactly. We've become a stronghold of resistance, a place where we can prepare ourselves and others for the challenges to come. Our alliance with the aliens has been invaluable in this endeavour. And now, you're a part of it, Bubba. You hold the key to even greater possibilities."

Bubba was taken aback by the revelations. It was clear that the Alien Base was not only a sanctuary but a center of resistance against Dr. Scorch's oppressive technology. The humans here had found a way to protect themselves, and Bubba's role in this grand scheme was becoming clearer.

With newfound purpose and determination, Bubba realized that his journey was not just about survival but about leading the charge against the impending threat. He turned to Tyro, ready to embrace his role in this epic struggle to protect humanity and Earth.

Bubba's mind raced as he recalled the events that had led him to this moment. The activation of the computer in Broad's Lab, the deactivation of the USD machine, and the subsequent disappearance of its effects on humans had brought about a turning point. The memories of his previous identity as Hubris and his connection to the mission involving the Black Dots came flooding back.

But there was something more pressing on Bubba's mind. He had an urgent desire to find Cletus. The enigmatic scientist had played a pivotal role in his transformation from Hubris to Bubba, and Bubba felt a deep connection with him. He couldn't shake the feeling that Cletus might be somewhere in the Alien Base.

As Bubba pondered these thoughts, a strange insect landed on his neck and delivered a sharp bite. At first, he winced in pain, but then he realized that this bite had a purpose. With the third bite, he experienced a sudden rush of memories that had previously eluded him.

The memories rushed in like a torrent, revealing the hidden layers of his past and his role as Hubris. He remembered the temple where he had first met Tyro, the complex mission involving the Black Dots, and the importance of locating Cletus.

Determined to find answers and reconnect with his past, Bubba turned to Tyro. "Tyro, I need to find Cletus. I remember now, he's a crucial part of all this. Can you help me locate him? I have questions that only he can answer."

Bubba noticed the emotions welling up in Tyro's eyes as they discussed finding Cletus. He saw a deep sadness within his friend and couldn't help but inquire gently, "Tyro, what's wrong? You seem really emotional about this. Is there

something you're not telling me?"

Tyro sighed heavily and began to open up about his father. "Bubba, you've just reminded me of something I've been trying to forget. My father, Dr. Cletus, was a brilliant scientist, and he's the one who discovered the connection between the invisible soil in the tube and this Alien Base."

Bubba could sense the pain in Tyro's voice and placed a reassuring hand on his shoulder. "I'm here for you, Tyro. You don't have to go through this alone. Tell me more about your father."

Tyro continued, "Dr. Scorch captured my father and has been keeping him in custody for a long time. It's not just imprisonment; Cletus is being used to manipulate the invisible soil, which, in turn, has a connection to this base. He's in a terrible condition, Bubba. He's been suffering for years."

Bubba felt a mix of sorrow and determination. "We have to rescue him, Tyro. We can't let Dr. Scorch continue to use your father in this way. I promise you, we'll find a way to set him free."

Tears welled up in Tyro's eyes as he looked at Bubba with gratitude. "Thank you, Bubba. You're a true friend. Let's work together to save my father and uncover the truth about the Black Dots mission."

As they shared this solemn moment, Bubba and Tyro forged an unbreakable bond, determined to rescue Dr. Cletus and bring an end to the suffering caused by Dr. Scorch's cruel manipulation.

The alarm in the Alien Base blared loudly, its urgent wailing piercing the air. People and creatures of all kinds, humans, sea creatures, and aliens, sprinted towards the shore. Bubba and Tyro joined the rush of excitement and anxiety, not entirely sure what had triggered this momentous event.

As they reached the shore, their eyes filled with wonder and tears as they beheld the incredible sight before them. A group of humans and aliens was returning from a mission, and with them, they carried the precious tube that held Dr. Cletus. The entire base erupted in jubilant cheers, joyous cries, and exuberant applause. It was a moment of unity and celebration that transcended boundaries and species.

Bubba turned to Tyro, whose eyes glistened with emotion. "Tyro, this is amazing! Look at the happiness on everyone's faces. Your father is coming back, and it's all because of the collaboration between humans and aliens."

Tyro's voice quivered with emotion as he responded, "Bubba, I can't believe this is happening. My father, Cletus, has been suffering for so long. It's the people here, the humans and aliens working together, who made this rescue possible. They are true heroes."

The jubilation continued around them as the group approached, carrying the tube containing Dr. Cletus. With careful precision and the aid of advanced technology, they began the process of reviving him. Bubba and Tyro watched with bated breath, the weight of the moment pressing upon them.

As Cletus's body began to show signs of life, Tyro couldn't contain his tears. He turned to Bubba, his voice choked with emotion. "Bubba, this is the day I thought I might never see. My father is coming back to us. Thank you for being here with me through all of this. I can't express how much it means to me."

Bubba smiled through his own tears and placed a hand on Tyro's shoulder. "Tyro, we're in this together. Your father's return is a testament to the power of collaboration and the resilience of the human spirit. Let's be there to welcome him back and to celebrate this incredible moment."

And as Dr. Cletus took his first breath in years, the base resounded with the cheers and applause of humans, aliens, and sea creatures alike. It was a moment of triumph, a symbol of unity, and a reminder that together, they could overcome any challenge, no matter how formidable.

As the group returned to the base with the still-unconscious Dr. Cletus, the celebratory atmosphere was palpable, but there was one crucial step left in the process of his revival. The tube that held Cletus could only be opened with the help of Bubba and the Heart of the ocean, the

crystal he had carefully kept in his pocket.

Amid the cheers and applause, Bubba took a deep breath, his heart pounding with anticipation. He reached into his pocket and retrieved the glittering Heart of the ocean. The crystal seemed to pulse with a life of its own as if it sensed the momentous task at hand.

Bubba approached the tube, Tyro and the gathered crowd looking on with hope and faith. With a steady hand, he touched the Heart of the ocean to the tube's surface. The crystal emitted a soft, ethereal glow as it interfaced with the tube's advanced technology.

The tube began to hiss, its mechanisms unlocking with precision. Slowly and with great care, the lid of the tube lifted, revealing the still-unconscious form of Dr. Cletus. It was a moment of collective relief, and the base fell into a reverent hush as they awaited the awakening of the scientist who held the key to so many mysteries.

Cletus's breathing remained steady, but he had not yet regained consciousness. The base's inhabitants held their breath, hopeful for what the future would bring now that he had been freed from the clutches of Dr. Scorch.

Dr. Cletus, a brilliant scientist and inventor, had pioneered a groundbreaking technology known as the "Thoughtter." The name "Thoughtter" was a combination of "thoughts" and "plotter," signifying its unique ability to translate the intricate patterns of human thought into a tangible and comprehensible form.

The Thoughtter was not just a machine; it was a marvel of ingenuity. It could intercept and record the frequencies generated by Dr. Cletus's thoughts, collecting the complex patterns and encoding them into a visual or auditory format. This technology opened up unprecedented possibilities for the exchange of knowledge and ideas between humans and aliens, as it could bridge the gap of communication by directly tapping into the innermost thoughts of an individual.

Rescuing Dr. Cletus from the clutches of Dr. Scorch had been a formidable task that involved the dedicated efforts of both humans and aliens. The alliance between these two species was further cemented by their shared commitment to bringing Cletus back to the world he had been separated from for so long.

The Thoughtter was not only a symbol of Dr. Cletus's remarkable intellect but also a beacon of hope. Its potential applications were boundless, and with the scientist's return, the collaborative efforts of humans and aliens could continue, with the Thoughtter as their bridge to understanding and shared progress.

As Dr. Cletus remained in his unconscious state, the base inhabitants knew that the inventor of the Thoughtter held the key to unlocking new frontiers of knowledge, understanding, and collaboration. They were determined to nurse him back to health and celebrate the reunion that would lead to a brighter future for all.

CHAPTER NINE

BUBBA'S LAST STAND

Inside the lab, two doctors, Dr. Marcus Grayson and Dr. Eleanor Wells, huddled over the unconscious body of Cletus. They had been trying to revive him, but his condition remained critical. The room was filled with a sense of urgency, as they knew that time was running out.

Dr. Grayson, a scientist driven by ambition and power, turned to Dr. Wells, his voice laced with frustration. "Dr. Wells, we've tried everything to wake him up, but nothing seems to be working. We need to find a solution, and quickly. Cletus's knowledge is vital to our research."

Dr. Wells, who had a deep understanding of the connection between Bubba and Cletus, replied with determination, "I've been thinking, Dr. Grayson. There might be a way to revive Cletus, but it involves using Bubba's blood sample. We know that the two of them share a unique connection." Dr. Grayson frowned, sceptical but intrigued. "Bubba's blood sample? How can that help?"

Dr. Wells explained, "Bubba's transformation was tied to Cletus's research, and their bond is stronger than we realized. If we infuse Cletus with Bubba's blood, it might jumpstart his system. But we must act quickly."

Dr. Grayson hesitated, torn between his desire for power and the urgency of the situation. After a moment of contemplation, he nodded. "Very well, let's proceed with your plan. We can't afford to lose Cletus. He's the key to unlocking the full potential of our research."

The two doctors swiftly prepared to obtain a sample of Bubba's blood. They knew that this desperate gamble might be the only way to save Cletus and harness his knowledge for their own gain. But little did they know that their actions would set into motion a chain of events that would challenge the very foundation of their mission and bring about a reckoning that would change the course of their destinies.

As Dr. Marcus Grayson and Dr. Eleanor Wells hurriedly prepared to obtain a sample of Bubba's blood, the urgency of the situation weighed heavily on their minds. Cletus's body lay in the open tube, exposed to the invisible soil that had sustained him for years. The transparent soil was beginning to lose its potential, and a growing sense of urgency filled the room.

Dr. Wells's voice was tinged with concern as she explained, "Dr. Grayson, we don't have much time. The invisible soil is losing its properties now that the tube is open. Once it turns completely opaque, it will become rock solid and swallow Cletus's body permanently."

Dr. Grayson nodded, realizing the gravity of the situation. "We must act swiftly, then. Bubba's blood may be the only way to revive Cletus and prevent the loss of his valuable knowledge."

With a sense of determination, they carefully extracted a sample of Bubba's blood and began the process of infusing it into Cletus's system. The room was filled with tension as they monitored every detail of the procedure, knowing that the fate of Cletus and the future of their research depended on its success. As the seconds ticked away and the transparent soil continued its transformation, the room grew even more fraught with urgency. The time was running out, and the two doctors could only hope that their desperate gamble would be enough to bring Cletus back from the brink before it was too late.

As Bubba prepared to offer his blood to revive Cletus, his thoughts were overwhelmed by the loving memories of his family. In the hologram display, he watched the live stream of his parents, Morvane and Nerissa, who were engaged in a heartfelt conversation about their son's future. Their voices were filled with joy and affection, creating a bittersweet blend of emotions within Bubba.

Morvane spoke with pride, "Nerissa, can you believe our boy has come so far? His intelligence and courage amaze me every day. He's destined for great things, I just know it."

Nerissa, her eyes shimmering with love, replied, "I couldn't agree more, Morvane. Our Bubba is a remarkable young man. I have no doubt he'll make us even prouder in the years to come." Bubba's heart swelled with warmth as he listened to their words. His bond with his parents was unbreakable, and their unwavering support had carried him through the most challenging of times.

But in the midst of his emotional reverie, Bubba's initial attempt to offer his blood was unsuccessful. His deep connection to his family and the memories of their love had temporarily disrupted the process. He needed to detach from these emotions in order to complete the procedure successfully.

As he made a second attempt, a sense of determination washed over him. He focused his thoughts on the immediate task at hand, suppressing the overwhelming emotions tied to his parents. This time, the blood flowed smoothly into the transfusion equipment, giving them hope that it would work.

However, as the procedure continued, an unexpected and alarming event occurred in the live stream. Bubba's image suddenly disappeared from the hologram display. Morvane and Nerissa, who had been engaged in joyful

conversation, exchanged panicked glances.

Nerissa cried out, "Bubba? Where did he go? He was just there."

Morvane's voice trembled as he called out, "Bubba! Can you hear us?"

The once joyful atmosphere of the live stream turned tense and anxious as Morvane and Nerissa desperately began to search for their missing son. Bubba watched in helplessness, his own emotions echoing the panic of his parents. The unexpected disappearance added a new layer of uncertainty and urgency to the already critical situation, leaving everyone in the lab on edge.

Dr. Marcus Grayson and Dr. Eleanor Wells emerged from the lab, their faces bearing the weight of the critical decision they had just made. They urgently called Tyro over to a quiet corner of the base, away from the prying eyes and ears of others. Tyro, his anxiety palpable, looked at them with a mixture of hope and fear. "What did you find? Is there a way to save my father?" Dr. Grayson, his voice laced with emotional urgency, spoke first. "Tyro, there's a unique reaction occurring in Bubba's heart. It's something we've never seen before, and we believe it may hold the key to reviving Cletus. But, it's a dangerous and untested procedure, and there's no guarantee of success."

Dr. Wells, her eyes filled with compassion, added, "In order to save Cletus, Bubba will have to make a tremendous sacrifice. We need a sample of his heart's reaction to conduct the procedure. But, Tyro, it's a high-risk endeavour, and it could cost Bubba his life."

Tyro's emotions swirled within him as he grappled with the gravity of the situation. His father, Cletus, was in danger, and his friend, Bubba, was now facing the possibility of sacrificing his life to save him.

He thought of the bond he had formed with Bubba and the unwavering support Bubba had shown to him throughout their journey. But he also couldn't bear the thought of losing his father, the one who had always believed in him and his potential. In a quivering voice, Tyro finally spoke, "I can't lose either of them. Bubba is my friend, and Cletus is my father. I need some time to think. Please, just give me a little time to decide."

Dr. Grayson and Dr. Wells nodded, understanding the weight of the decision Tyro had to make. "Take your time, Tyro. We'll be here when you're ready. But please, understand that time is running out for Cletus."

With that, they left Tyro to grapple with the impossible decision that lay ahead, his heart heavy with the knowledge that he might have to choose between the two most important people in his life.

Alone with the Thoughtter, Tyro was caught in the whirlwind of emotions and decisions. He stared at the strange patterns being plotted, realizing that they were emanating from Bubba's thoughts. It was as though his friend, who was preparing to make the ultimate sacrifice, was trying to communicate with him in a way that words could not express.

The holographic patterns danced before Tyro's eyes, and he began to decipher the intricate code that Bubba was creating with his thoughts. In the silence of the moment, he felt an intense connection with his friend, a connection that transcended words and actions.

As Tyro pieced together the pattern, he could sense the depth of Bubba's inner conflict, the love and devotion he felt for his family and his desire to save Cletus. It was a message of selflessness and bravery, a testament to the remarkable character of his friend.

In the midst of this silent conversation, Tyro found himself wrestling with his own inner turmoil. He questioned whether he could bear the loss of either his father, Cletus, or his loyal friend, Bubba. The weight of the choice ahead seemed almost unbearable.

With tears in his eyes, Tyro spoke softly to himself, "I can't let them down. Bubba is willing to sacrifice himself for Cletus, and my father's life hangs in the balance. I need to find a way to save them both."

The Thoughtter continued to plot the patterns, a silent reminder of the immense courage and sacrifice that Bubba was willing to undertake. It was a moment of deep introspection for Tyro, and he knew that the decision he made would shape the fate of those he held most dear.

Tyro retreated to a secret chamber tucked away from prying eyes, the weight of the world on his shoulders. Inside the chamber, he carefully accessed a small device that was discreetly embedded at the nape of his neck. With a swift motion, he activated it, and in an instant, Tyro found himself transported into a surreal machine known as the "Infineighteen."

This remarkable invention, created by Tyro himself, held the power to enter the minds of others and manipulate their thoughts within mere seconds. The only condition was that the subject must be lying on the transparent soil inside the tube. Tyro's discovery had been a joint effort with his father, Cletus, a collaboration that had been cut short when Cletus was taken into custody by Dr. Scorch.

Inside the Infineighteen, Tyro could navigate through the intricacies of a person's mind, a place filled with memories, emotions, and desires. He had used this technology for various purposes, but now, the situation was more dire than ever.

As Tyro prepared to use the Infineighteen, he couldn't help but think of Cletus and Bubba. The memories of their shared work on this invention, the laughter they had shared, and the hopes they had held for the future flooded his mind. It was a reminder of the bond he shared with both of them, a bond that he was now determined to protect at any cost.

Tyro knew that he had a unique opportunity to enter Bubba's mind, to understand the depth of his friend's thoughts, and to potentially influence the decision that lay ahead. With a deep breath, he initiated the sequence and entered the intricate maze of Bubba's consciousness.

As Tyro ventured into the labyrinth of Bubba's mind, he was acutely aware of the time constraint imposed by the Infineighteen machine. It had the power to delve into the depths of a person's thoughts for a mere eighteen minutes, a window of opportunity that was both a blessing and a curse. Intriguingly, the Infineighteen came with a dire consequence. Any person who used it to infiltrate another's mind and overstayed their welcome in the domain of thoughts would find themselves wandering into the treacherous territories known as the "forgetting cells." This perilous realm had the power to erase one's very existence, leading to a fate that could only be described as a form of psychological death.

For Tyro, this added an element of urgency to his mission. He needed to navigate the labyrinth of Bubba's consciousness, understand his friend's inner turmoil, and influence his decision in a way that would save both Bubba and Cletus, all within the tight confines of the eighteen-minute limit. The clock was ticking, and

Tyro knew that every second counted as he journeyed deeper into the recesses of Bubba's mind, fully aware of the life-or-death stakes involved.

Inside the intricate landscapes of Bubba's mind, Tyro and Bubba's consciousnesses stood face to face. The digital clock within the Infineighteen machine reminded them of the ticking seconds as they engaged in a deeply emotional conversation.

Tears welled in Tyro's eyes as he pleaded with his friend, "Bubba, you can't do this. I can't lose you. Cletus is important, but so are you. You mean everything to me."

Bubba, his own eyes misty, tried to convince Tyro, "Tyro, Cletus has the knowledge that can change the world. My life is just one among many, but your father's work could benefit countless lives. This is the right choice."

Tyro shook his head, his voice trembling, "Both of you are important. I can't bear to lose either of you."

In the background, the Infineighteen machine's clock continued to count down the minutes.

Bubba reached out and held Tyro's hand, his grip steady and full of sincerity. "Listen, Tyro, if I don't make it out of this, promise me you'll tell my parents that I love them. Tell them I did this for a better world and for you, my dearest friend."

Tyro nodded, tears streaming down his cheeks. "I promise, Bubba. But let's find another way, together. We'll save both you and my father."

Bubba smiled weakly, his voice filled with warmth, "That's the spirit, Tyro. Never give up. Now, use the time we have left to help Cletus. I believe in you, my friend."

As the seconds dwindled, Bubba sent one last heartfelt message through Tyro. In the real world, the Infineighteen machine began to shut down, and Bubba's consciousness prepared to leave Tyro's mind.

With a final embrace, Bubba whispered to Tyro, "Tell my parents that I love them and that I'll be with them in spirit. And remember, my friend, you're never alone. You have the strength to save us all."

As the Infineighteen timer reached zero, Bubba's consciousness began to fade, leaving Tyro with the weight of the world on his shoulders and a promise to fulfil for his dear friend. As Tyro returned from the depths of Bubba's consciousness, he was met by the two doctors, Dr. Marcus Grayson and Dr. Eleanor Wells. Their faces were a mix of concern and anticipation, as they had just completed the delicate procedure

involving Bubba's heart.

Breathless and emotionally drained, Tyro struggled to find words. He explained, "I was inside Bubba's mind, and he made a sacrifice... a selfless one. I couldn't let him go through with it."

The doctors exchanged a glance, understanding the gravity of the situation. Dr. Grayson spoke softly, "Tyro, we had to proceed with the procedure. We removed Bubba's heart and used the sample to revive Cletus. It was our only chance to save him."

Tyro felt a heavy pang of guilt and sadness as he rushed to the lab where Cletus and Bubba's bodies were kept. He approached Bubba's lifeless form and placed a trembling hand on his friend's forehead. Tears welled up in his eyes as he whispered a heartfelt, "Thank you, Bubba, for your sacrifice. I'm so sorry."

The room was filled with a sombre atmosphere, Tyro's grief palpable. His heart ached for the loss of his dear friend. But just as he was coming to terms with the sacrifice, a gentle touch on his shoulder made him turn around.

It was Cletus, his father, who had woken up from his long sleep. The look in Cletus's eyes was a mixture of gratitude, love, and relief. He placed a hand on Tyro's shoulder, and his voice was filled with emotion as he said, "Thank you, my son, for bringing me back. And thank you for your unwavering friendship with Bubba. He made the ultimate sacrifice, and I promise that we will honour his memory."

In that poignant moment, the room was charged with a profound sense of loss and renewal. Bubba's sacrifice had given Cletus a second chance at life, and Tyro's courage had bridged the gap between despair and hope. It was a testament to the strength of their bonds and the lengths they were willing to go to protect and save one another. As Cletus marvelled at his son's discovery of the Infineighteen, a spark of hope lit up in his eyes. He couldn't help but ask the pressing question, "Tyro, how much time has passed since Bubba's heart was disconnected from his body?" The two doctors, Dr. Marcus Grayson and Dr. Eleanor Wells, stepped forward to provide an answer. Dr. Grayson spoke with a hint of optimism, "Cletus, it's been just a matter of minutes since the procedure. We had to act quickly to save you, and the timing was critical."

Cletus nodded, processing the information. A determined expression crossed his face, and he turned to Tyro with unwavering resolve. "If there's still time, I believe I can use the Infineighteen to enter Bubba's mind and save him as well. We must act swiftly."

Tyro's eyes widened with surprise and hope. The possibility of saving Bubba, his dear friend, was a ray of light in the midst of their recent loss. He couldn't contain his excitement and gratitude. "You can do that, Dad? That's incredible!" Cletus nodded, his heart filled with determination. "With the Infineighteen, I believe we can bridge the connection between our minds and save Bubba. But time is of the essence. Let's proceed."

With renewed hope and a sense of urgency, Cletus, Tyro, and the two doctors prepared for the next phase of their extraordinary journey, knowing that they had a chance to bring back the friend who had made the ultimate sacrifice.

CHAPTER TEN

RISING FROM THE ASHES

Dr. Cletus had been working tirelessly on the mysterious chip for months before getting captured by Dr Scorch, the culmination of a lifetime of research. He knew that its activation was the key to saving Bubba's life and returning him to his family. As he stood in front of the imposing machine known as "Infineighteen," a hushed anticipation filled the room. His son Tyro, with a worried look on his face, watched his father's every move.

Dr. Cletus: (murmuring to himself) "It's now or never. This chip holds the answer to everything."

With a steady hand, Dr. Cletus gently inserted the chip into a port at the base of Infineighteen. As he activated it, the machine hummed to life, emitting an eerie, otherworldly glow. The room seemed to vibrate with an energy that was palpable.

Tyro: (anxiously) "Father, are you sure about this? It seems so... risky."

Dr. Cletus: (looking back at his son) "I've spent my entire life researching this, Tyro. It's the only chance we have to save Bubba and understand what's happening to him. Now, stand back."

Just as Dr. Cletus finished speaking, there was a deafening "bing bang" sound effect, and he collapsed to the floor, unconscious. Panic filled the room as Tyro rushed to his father's side.

Tyro: (frantically) "Dad! Dad, can you hear me? Someone, help!"

Other doctors, including Dr. Grayson and Dr. Wells, quickly rushed to the scene, and they managed to carry Dr. Cletus to a nearby bed. As he lay there, unconscious, Tyro knew he had to stay strong. His father had given clear instructions for this critical moment.

Tyro: (determined, addressing the doctors) "Listen up, everyone. We need to proceed with Bubba's heart surgery immediately. My father prepared for this. You know what to do. I'll stay with him and monitor his condition." The other doctors, including Dr. Grayson and Dr. Wells, nodded, and with a sense of urgency, they began preparing for the delicate procedure to fix Bubba's heart within his body.

Dr. Grayson: (focused) "We don't have a second to waste. Prep the operating room and get the equipment ready."

Dr. Wells: (checking the equipment) "His vital signs are weakening. We need to act fast.

As the doctors prepared for surgery, Tyro turned his attention back to his unconscious father, whispering words of encouragement.

Tyro: (softly) "You've trained us well, Dad. We'll save Bubba and you. Just like you said, we have eighteen minutes. We won't let you down."

The countdown had begun. In the race against time, the fate of both Bubba and Dr. Cletus hung in the balance.

As Dr. Cletus delved into Bubba's thoughts, he found himself in an intricate maze of memories and emotions. It was a daunting task to navigate through the complex neural pathways, but he was determined. After what seemed like an eternity, he finally located the limbic system, the emotional center of Bubba's brain.

Dr. Cletus: (whispering to himself) "I've found it. Now, to establish the connection and stabilize it."

Cletus gently initiated contact with the limbic system. It responded with a series of vivid, fragmented memories. He could see snippets of Bubba's life, from childhood adventures to moments of happiness and sorrow.

Meanwhile, in the operating room, Dr. Grayson and Dr. Wells worked with precision and determination to repair Bubba's damaged heart. The room was filled with the soft hum of medical equipment and the focused voices of the surgical team.

Dr. Grayson: (concentrated) "Scalpel, please."

Nurse: "Scalpel coming right up, Dr. Grayson."

With a steady hand, Dr. Grayson continued the delicate procedure, while Dr. Wells monitored Bubba's vital signs.

Dr. Wells: (calmly) "Steady on the heart rate.

Good. We're making progress."

Back in the room where Dr. Cletus was connected to Bubba's mind, Tyro watched over his father's unconscious body, feeling a mix of anxiety and hope.

Tyro: (softly to himself) "Hang in there, Dad. You've got this. Bubba's heart surgery is going well, and you're inside his mind, doing your part."

Time was of the essence. The clock was ticking, and they all knew they had only eighteen minutes to save both Bubba and Dr. Cletus. It was a race against time, but with determination, skill, and a father's unwavering love, they were determined to succeed.

As Tyro kept a watchful eye on his unconscious father, Dr. Cletus, he was alerted by a strange sound emanating from the Thoughtter machine. The readings on the machine's display indicated a shift in Bubba's mind frequencies. Tyro quickly realized that it was a message from his father. Tyro: (excited) "A message from Dad? What's going on in there?"

He deciphered the message and, just like in Bubba's mind, a holographic projection of Bubba's parents, Nerissa and Morvane, appeared in the room, with Bubba's replicates engaging in the heart-warming interaction.

Nerissa: (smiling) "Bubba, my dear, can you hear us? It's Mom and Dad."

Morvane: (grinning) "We're here with you, son."

The holographic figures of Bubba's parents felt so real that Tyro couldn't help but be moved by the emotional connection.

Tyro: (with a lump in his throat) "This is incredible. Mom, Dad, Bubba's talking to you."

Nerissa: (with warmth) "We're here for him, Tyro. We've missed our son so much."

Morvane: (with pride) "He's a fighter, just like his old man. We'll be reunited soon."

Tyro couldn't help but shed a tear of relief. The live stream connection provided a lifeline for both Bubba and Dr. Cletus, and it was a profound moment that united the family in a way that transcended the boundaries of consciousness.

Tyro: (emotionally) "Thank you, Dad, for this connection. Bubba needed to see Mom and Dad. It's giving him strength."

With Bubba's replicates engaging in heartfelt conversations with the holographic images of his parents, Tyro felt a renewed sense of determination to ensure that the heart surgery went smoothly. The combined efforts of his father and the surgical team were their best hope for bringing Bubba back to his family, where he truly belonged.

Bubba found himself sitting on the tranquil shores of a crystal-clear lake within the vast landscape of his mind. The gentle lapping of the water against the shore was soothing. As he took in the serenity of the moment, his father, Morvane, approached, a warm smile on his face.

Morvane: (with a gentle tone) "Bubba, my boy, it's been quite a journey, hasn't it?"

Bubba: (nodding) "It has, Dad. I've been through
so much."

Morvane: (sitting beside him) "Life can be like these waters, Bubba. Sometimes calm, sometimes turbulent. But it's in these moments of stillness that we often find clarity."

Bubba looked out at the peaceful waters, absorbing the wisdom in his father's words.

Bubba: (curious) "What's the secret, Dad? How do you find meaning in all of this?"

Morvane: (reflective) "Well, son, life isn't just about what you get; it's about what you give. The true meaning lies in the connections you make, the love you share, and the impact you have on others."

Bubba's eyes glistened as he listened to his father.

Bubba: (thoughtful) "I've learned that too, Dad, through all of this."

Morvane: (nodding) "That's my boy. The way of giving, of selflessness, that's where true satisfaction lies. When you can make a difference in someone's life, it's the most rewarding thing."

Bubba: (feeling grateful) "I've seen the love and care from so many people, including you and Mom. It's what's kept me going."

Morvane: (smiling proudly) "And you've also learned the way of resilience, courage, and determination, Bubba. Those are equally important."

As they continued their heartfelt conversation on the shores of Bubba's mind, Bubba felt a profound sense of connection with his father. He understood that life's meaning was not just about what one could attain for oneself, but about the impact they could make on the world and the lives of those they touched.

Bubba: (feeling content) "Thank you, Dad. I'm so lucky to have your guidance, even in moments like this."

Morvane: (with a loving embrace) "And I'm lucky to have a son as strong and compassionate as you, Bubba. We'll get through this, together."

The conversation between father and son on the shores of Bubba's mind was a powerful reminder of the enduring strength of their bond and the profound life lessons they shared. It gave Bubba the strength he needed to face the challenges ahead and to emerge from his ordeal with a deeper understanding of life's true meaning.

As Bubba sat by the serene lakeshore, his heart warmed even more when he felt a gentle presence behind him. Turning around, he saw his mother, Nerissa, with a loving smile on her face. She sat down beside Bubba, and he could feel the warmth of her embrace.

Nerissa: (tenderly) "Oh, my precious Bubba. It's been so long since I've held you like this."

Bubba: (teary-eyed) "Mom, I've missed you more than words can express."

Nerissa gently wiped away a tear from Bubba's cheek.

Nerissa: (with affection) "I've been with you every step of the way, my love. Even when I couldn't be by your side, my heart was always with you."

Bubba: (feeling comforted) "I've felt your presence, Mom. It's what's kept me going."

Nerissa's eyes twinkled with love and maternal pride.

Nerissa: (softly) "You're the embodiment of our love, Bubba. You have strength and a spirit that's touched the hearts of so many."

Bubba: (humbled) "I've learned so much from both of you, Mom and Dad. Life's meaning, the power of giving, and the strength of family."

Nerissa: (embracing him) "We're so proud of the person you've become. And we're here to support you, just as we always have been."

The three of them, Bubba, his father Morvane, and his mother Nerissa, sat by the lakeshore, sharing a moment of love, affection, and unbreakable family bonds.

Bubba: (with gratitude) "I feel so blessed to have you both as my parents. Your love is my anchor." Nerissa: (holding him close) "And your strength is our inspiration, Bubba. We're here to guide you through this, every step of the way."

In this profound moment, the power of family, love, and unity became even more evident. As Bubba faced the challenges ahead, he knew he had the unwavering support and love of his parents to help him through the journey of life.

Inside the mysterious temple, Bubba, now a seventy-five-year-old man, held the Stone fish in his hand. The temple had an aura of ancient wisdom and a sense of timelessness. As he touched the stone to his eyes, the world around him seemed to shift, and a profound understanding washed over him.

The faithful dog that had been his companion barked joyfully, sensing the transformation occurring within Bubba. To Bubba's amazement, he began to understand the dog's language. Tyro, the loyal canine, was just as surprised as his owner.

Bubba: (smiling) "Tyro, it's you! You've been with me all these years."

Tyro: (barking with excitement) "Bubba, it's really you! I've waited for you."

As Bubba communicated with Tyro, a flood of memories and stories rushed back to him. The bond they shared was not just one of companionship but of true friendship and understanding.

Bubba: (teary-eyed) "Tyro, what happened after all those years? Where did our journey take us?"

Tyro: (with a wagging tail) "We travelled to places far and wide, met countless people, and shared adventures together. You helped so many, Bubba."

As Tyro recounted their adventures, Bubba listened with a sense of fulfilment. He had spent his years making a difference in the lives of others, just as his parents had taught him in the depths of his mind.

Bubba: (grateful) "Tyro, it's been a remarkable journey, hasn't it?"

Tyro: (with a wise look) "It has, Bubba. And now, you've unlocked a new chapter of understanding. The temple has revealed its secrets to you." Bubba felt a deep sense of gratitude for the experiences he had shared with Tyro, for the wisdom the temple had bestowed upon him, and for the enduring love of his parents. As they sat together in the mysterious temple, Bubba's journey through life continued, filled with new possibilities and newfound understanding.

For the sake of clarity, let's recap the sequence of events leading to this point:

Bubba, a close friend of Dr. Cletus's son Tyro, had undergone the successful heart surgery with Dr. Grayson and Dr. Wells' expert care. Dr. Cletus had ventured into Bubba's mind to provide him with the mental strength needed to endure the surgery, even though he wasn't Bubba's father. His friendship and dedication to Bubba were equally unwavering.

As the surgical procedure concluded successfully, Bubba emerged from it in stable condition. Tyro, relieved beyond measure, was there to welcome his friend back to the world with a heartfelt embrace. The joy of their reunion was palpable, and Bubba was now on the road to recovery. Meanwhile, Dr. Cletus, who had helped Bubba from within his mind, returned to his base after the surgery's success. He had demonstrated the incredible power of love, dedication, and human spirit in the face of adversity.

As for Dr. Scorch, the villain who had posed a threat, Dr. Cletus had dealt a decisive blow. He destroyed the entire system of Dr. Scorch and, in a dramatic confrontation, defeated the malevolent aliens who had allied with Scorch. In a surprising twist, the alien villain Scorch, recognizing the error of his ways, joined forces with Dr. Cletus, a sign of redemption and hope for the future.

With Bubba saved and Dr. Scorch's threat eliminated, Dr. Cletus stood as a symbol of love, determination, and the enduring power of the human spirit. The story had come full circle, and the characters had found their resolutions in the face of adversity.

Conclusion

In the face of adversity, the strength of the human spirit, the bonds of love, and the power of redemption shine brightly. Bubba, a friend in need, found himself in a perilous situation, but the unwavering support of those around him, especially Dr. Cletus, made all the difference.

Through the interconnected efforts of a father's love, skilled doctors, and the tenacity of a loyal friend, Bubba's life was saved. The mysterious temple, the healing power of thoughts, and the unity of the human and alien worlds added a touch of the extraordinary to this incredible journey.

In the end, this story is a testament to the indomitable nature of the human spirit, the capacity to give and support others in their times of need, and the potential for redemption and transformation even in the most unexpected places. It serves as a reminder that, no matter the challenges faced, love, dedication, and the strength of character can lead to a triumphant resolution.

About The Author

In his career as an **Automobile Engineer, Former Head of the Department**, Automobile Engineering (Polytechnic) and **Computer Science Faculty** (High School), **Maheshwara Shastri** has contributed his skills to several private companies, Colleges and Schools in India. Hailing from a simple family structure, he has shared his life journey with his mother, wife, and two sisters, having lost his father at an early age.

However, beneath the surface of his professional life, Maheshwara Shastri harbours a deep passion for storytelling. He always aspired to be an author, initially penning short stories that carried profound moral lessons about life. His creativity knows no bounds, and he often immerses himself in the realms of his imagination, where he dreams, travels, and translates the vivid landscapes of his mind into the pages of his books. What started as a mere hobby has now blossomed into a full-fledged profession.

As a dreamer and visionary, Maheshwara Shastri firmly believes that dreams, when pursued relentlessly, can materialize into reality. Among his aspirations is to create his own animation movies, and he envisions establishing his very own animation movie studio.

Currently, Maheshwara Shastri is in the process of crafting two intriguing books. One is titled **'Being Honest Will Cost You Everything'** delving into the harsh realities that honesty often unveils. The second is **'Peace Piece'** which explores the profound consequences of consciousness.

Maheshwara Shastri's writing often revolves around the theme of self-belief and the untapped potential that resides within each of us. He emphasizes that our unique abilities are a treasure trove that cannot be taken from us. By recognizing and nurturing these talents, we can master the art of living.

In addition to his current projects, Maheshwara Shastri has authored several other books, including

ENGLISH BOOKS

- 'Black Dots'
- 'Shores of Wonder'
- 'Out of Arena: The Mysterious Land of Life'
- 'Turns & Twists in the Dreams of God'
- 'Meal - The Manager'
- 'Precision of Pre Decision'

KANNADA BOOKS

- 'Saavinaache Payana'
- 'Naa Obba Writtarru – Baa Guru Pustaka Odu'
- 'Kanakaambari Kathe'

His body of work reflects his passion for storytelling and his commitment to inspiring others through his literary creations.

Author Communication Address
Maheshwara Shastri, #71, 1st Floor, 1st Main, 2nd Cross, Chamundeshwari Layout, Vidyaranyapura, Bengaluru 560097
Write to - mahesh.thm@gmail.com
Chat - +91 94819 70964 (Whats App)

Declaration Of Fictional Content

This book, its characters, and the events portrayed within its pages are entirely products of the author's imagination and are intended for entertainment purposes. Any similarities to real-life individuals, situations, or events are purely coincidental. The author wishes to emphasize that this work is a work of fiction, and any resemblance to actual persons, living or deceased, or real-life events is unintentional.

The names, characters, and incidents in this book are the result of the author's creativity and should not be construed as factual. Any references to locations, organizations, or historical events are used fictitiously and are not intended to represent reality.

The author acknowledges that the real world is vast and diverse, and while inspiration can be drawn from it, this book is a piece of art and storytelling. Readers should approach its content with the understanding that it is entirely fictional and not meant to reflect or comment upon real-life situations, individuals, or events.

Signed,
[MAHESHWARA SHASTRI]
29.09.2023
Bengaluru, Karnataka, India